DESTROYER

The Bugging Out Series: Book Nine

NOAH MANN

ISBN-10: 1722668369
ISBN-13: 978-1722668365

Every dictator is an enemy of freedom,
an opponent of law.

Demosthenes

Part One

Prisoners

One

"Neil…"

I called softly to him after an hour of silence from his dim cell. He'd passed out after our initial interaction, wet breaths seeming almost ready to choke the life from him as he slept.

"Neil…"

He continued to sleep. And I continued to think.

How was it possible that my friend, my best friend, was here, just yards away, talking to me years after he'd been shot dead right before my eyes? I'd held his lifeless body in those moments, and had stood at the rectangular hole in the earth as his handmade casket was lowered in at Bandon's cemetery.

I was living in an impossibility. And yet, it was not just possible—it was real. It was fact.

Neil Moore was less than ten feet from me, as alive as I was.

"Neil…"

I noticed the first stirrings from him since exhaustion had dragged him down from the waking world. He shifted where he lay, responding to my voice. I hoped it was that which was beginning to rouse him. The connection we had once shared as the best of friends had been ended by his death, and I wanted it now to be rekindled by his inexplicable resurrection.

"Come on, wake up," I urged him quietly.

His head rose just a bit from where it had rested on his arm.

"Fletch..."

I scooted closer to the bars of the cell, just a few inches space between each. I tried to slip my arm through, to reach across the aisle that separated our enclosures, but it was a gesture of support at best. The distance to him was too great to cross, and my muscled forearm, toughened by the daily duties of surviving in a still recovering world, made it only past the wrist, leaving just my hand waving back and forth as I struggled to reach out toward my friend.

Finally I gave up and withdrew my hand, pressing my face against the bars instead, peering through the space between them.

"How are you?" I asked.

"I've been better," Neil answered.

He reached to the bars, gripping one with bony fingers and hauling himself slowly toward the barrier. It was night outside, and just as dark in our small part of the old bank building, but light from the guard's fire beyond the vault trickled in. Enough that I looked upon my friend's shadowed face with both sadness and fear.

"Worse than on our way back from Cheyenne?" Neil asked me, noting my silent reaction to his gaunt appearance.

I didn't know, though. That time, that journey, those obstacles had tested him, and Elaine, and me in ways none of us could have imagined. He was, I thought, referencing his lowest point. That brief moment when, on the brink of starvation, with sickness wracking his body, he had been forced to do what would have been inconceivable before the time when some chose cannibalism to survive. Neil had succumbed to necessity at that time, in that place, and he had survived.

Only to die again.

"You'll be okay," I told him.

He nodded weakly, his eyes closing briefly as his head bowed.

"It's been a long time," Neil said. "I didn't know if you were even alive. If anyone was still alive."

He was professing ignorance of the situation in the town he'd left so that it might be saved. But how could that be? Despite the folly of his dying before my eyes, I'd seen him on the broadcast from the Unified Government, with General Weatherly standing near his bound prisoner. He'd known then that we'd thwarted the siege of Bandon. That we'd driven the enemy off. He'd heard me trade Sheryl Quincy for him.

Yet he seemed as in the dark about what had become of our town as I was about his being alive.

"Neil, you have to tell me what happened."

His face rose again and he looked at me, puzzled.

"What do you mean?"

"I mean with Weatherly, and the trade for Sheryl, and..."

He scooted himself up to the bars, pressed against them now, his utterly confused gaze fixed upon me.

"Fletch, what are you talking about? What trade?"

What was happening? How could he be claiming no knowledge of the exchange I'd initiated, swapping his life for the traitor we'd discovered in our midst?

"You for Sheryl Quincy," I said.

Neil stared at me, his weary gaze narrowing with almost painful confusion. Still, I couldn't fathom how what he was experiencing could match my own lack of understanding at the moment.

"I don't know what you're talking about," my friend said.

I pressed myself close to the bars and fixed a hard gaze on him.

"Neil...I watched you die. You died in my arms."

Whatever shock he'd expressed to this point was more than matched by the reaction I saw on his face. He eased an inch or so back from the bars, his head turning a bit as he stared into the deeper darkness at the back of his cell. It seemed to me that he wasn't just reacting to what I'd just told him—he was processing it. Attempting to understand the impossibility. Except...

Except it appeared to me that my friend was not approaching that mental exercise from a place of expected failure. He was, instead, trying to fit known pieces into an unknown scenario. Pieces known only to him.

After a moment he turned back to face me, the confusion gone from his face. From his eyes. In its place was regret. And realization.

"Fletch, I'm so sorry. I—"

"Hello, gentlemen."

The voice interrupted our fledgling conversation. *His* voice.

"Have we become reacquainted?" Earl Perkins asked.

I looked into the aisle between our cells, to where that short corridor began at the entrance to the vault. Perkins stood there, long revolver holstered diagonally across the front of his belt, Sheryl and his apparent right-hand man, Bryce, at his side. Behind them, a key ring spinning on one finger, stood Jake, the man charged with guarding us.

"They've been doing some jawing, Earl," Jake said.

Both Bryce and Perkins turned to fix a disapproving gaze on the seemingly simple man charged with guarding us. He hadn't committed some unforgivable sin, but he clearly recognized that his transgression was not far from that.

"I mean Mr. Perkins," Jake corrected, humbling himself. "They've been talking a bit. Not a whole lot, but..."

Jake stopped, the uncomfortable attention directed at him muting any further narrative he could offer of the short time Neil and I had been together. Perkins and Bryce let their stares linger a few seconds longer, and in that brief span of time I noticed something. While attention had shifted to the man guarding us, one had not turned to look at him—Sheryl Quincy. The former Army private and forever traitor hadn't looked away from Neil and me.

From me specifically.

I couldn't judge the look she had fixed on me with any certainty. It wasn't overt anger or hatred. Nor was it pity. But it was something, with a hint of animus simmering just below the surface. It seemed odd, I thought, that any overt disgust would be reserved for me. I had been the one who'd seen to her trade for Neil.

For who I'd thought was Neil.

I was the reason she was free. The reason that she was here. Maybe, I thought, that outcome hadn't been all she'd hoped it would be.

That was wishful thinking, I realized. She'd thrown in with the Unified Government and had done the same with Perkins when the former was no longer a viable entity to align herself with. She was, I was coming to understand, a parasitic person, attaching herself to whichever power structure could most benefit her at the moment. That made her scum, in my eyes. It also made her dangerous.

I wondered if Earl Perkins realized just who, and what, he'd brought into his inner circle.

"Have you all gotten down to the meaty part, yet?" Perkins asked as he stepped closer, equidistant between the cells Neil and I occupied. "Well?"

I saw Neil's head dip a bit, as if he didn't want to acknowledge either the question, or the answer which would satisfy it.

"Utterly precious," Perkins said, nodding toward my friend. "He can't bring himself to clue you in."

My gaze shifted between our dictatorial captor and Neil. There was something known between them. Something shared that I was not privy to.

Yet.

"Too bad," Perkins said, clapping his hands together once with glee. "How about we play a game?"

Now Neil looked up, to Perkins first, then to me. All emotions on the darker side of human nature were present in his gaze right then—fear, apology, desperation most prevalent.

"Let's get them outside," Perkins said.

He turned, Sheryl taking hold of his hand as he stabbed it toward her, following him out.

"On your feet," Bryce said to me.

Next to him, Jake eased the double-barrel shotgun from where it was slung behind, leveling it at me.

"Any trouble, and Jake will give you each a barrel," Bryce cautioned as he took the key from our guard. "And that would mean you'd miss the fun to come."

I didn't know what that meant, but I was certain both Neil and I were about to find out.

Two

We were trussed up and led out into the night by Bryce and Jake, the pair marching us down the center of the street toward a large group of people lit by the dancing glow of flames leaping from steel barrels. They parted as we neared, enough that what lay beyond them—a flatbed truck placed in the intersection, Perkins standing atop it like the master of ceremonies upon a stage—became visible. As did the fact that the holstered revolver was now in his hand, held at his side, its long barrel reaching past the diminutive dictator's knee.

Twenty yards from the ominous gathering Neil stumbled, collapsing to his knees. I halted instinctively, but Bryce, who'd focused his attention on me, kept me moving with a solid jab from the stock of his Remington pump. Just behind us, Jake struggled to get my friend back on his feet.

"Time's a wasting!" Perkins shouted toward us, a chuckle rolling lightly through his assembled followers.

I chanced a quick look behind without slowing and saw Neil on his feet again, Jake propping him up with a grip on where his hands were bound behind his neck, using the 'angel wings' to march my friend forward.

My *living* friend.

The opportunity to probe Neil as to the impossibility of his presence hadn't fully presented itself. Just as I'd begun to lead him toward that subject our captors had appeared, interrupting what might have come. Looking forward again, to the truck where Perkins stood with his long revolver in hand, I began to wonder if answers were a luxury neither of us would have time to behold.

"Bring our guests up here!' Perkins shouted with smarmy glee.

His followers heeded his directive, dozens pouring from the crowd to grab Neil and me from our escorts and manhandle us up onto the truck's flat bed. Bryce climbed up and lashed us to a mesh of metalwork protecting the cab from any load behind. This wasn't the truck I'd been brought into town on, lacking the throne Perkins had sat in, but it was similar and appeared in working order. That the Yuma colony had at least two working vehicles, and likely more, was an impressive accomplishment considering their physical appearance. They were a driven, scrappy, tired collection of humanity. They were survivors.

And they wanted blood.

"Kill them!"

That was only one of the cries that rose from the crown surrounding where we'd been put on display upon the truck. More shouted out for us to be tortured in various ways. Burned alive. Drawn apart between vehicles. Chopped up with axes. Through it all, standing alone with us near, Perkins soaked in the fervor. As the fury built, he walked over to where Bryce had left Neil and me tied to the back of the cab, eyeing us from just a foot away.

"Do you hear that?" Perkins asked us, smiling. "Do you see that?"

It was impossible for us to not, and he knew that. It was, to him, a moment of glory we were witness to. His glory.

"*I* created this," Perkins gloated to us. "*I* made them. They will do *anything* for me. All I have to do is give them what they want."

Perkins stepped away from us and faced his people. They roared at him, fists pounding the air. One woman bolted from the group and tried to scramble aboard the flatbed, Bryce and Jake grabbing her before she could. As they pulled her away I could see in her eyes something more than hatred. More than fury.

I saw bloodlust.

She, and the others, had been promised all that they felt they been denied. Things that I'd received, and Neil, as well, when he'd been part of us. Part of Bandon.

When I'd first been hauled into town just hours earlier after the ambush which had killed Dave Arndt, I'd been received with quiet animus. Whatever had been held within had been released, summoned by Perkins in pursuit of his greater goal.

"Bandon will be ours!" he shouted, thrusting his revolver into the air.

I looked past him, to the nearly frothing crowd, sampling their belief in his promise. But just for a moment. My gaze found an island of calm among them—Sheryl Quincy.

She stood near the back of the truck, mixed in with the riled survivors, staring up at me. Something just short of a smile curling her lips slightly. There was anticipation in the expression. I was not eager to know what it was that was fueling that look about her.

But I was about to find out.

"These men represent Bandon," Perkins said, shifting the revolver toward us, its muzzle wide and threatening.

"Forty-four isn't a bad way to go," Neil said weakly.

I looked to him and nodded.

"I suppose not," I said. "I'd prefer a forty-five."

"God bless John Browning," Neil said, a hint of chuckle trailing off his offering of gallows humor.

"Gentlemen," Perkins said, drawing our attention as he stepped toward us again, leaving a few feet distance this time. "We're going to play a game."

With those words, I knew what was coming.

Perkins tipped the revolver upward and opened its cylinder, dumping a number of shells from the six shooter. He closed the cylinder and opened his palm, five fat .44 magnum rounds showing on its rough surface.

Next to me I sensed my friend straightening where he'd been bound. Since we'd been tied to the back of the truck's cab, he'd slouched severely, almost hanging from the bindings. He was incredibly weak, malnourishment and other horrors having wreaked havoc on his body. But he wasn't going to let Perkins do what he'd planned without facing the man straight on, standing tall, unafraid.

Neither was I.

The man noticed our defiant posture, his gaze shifting between us, whatever macabre joviality he'd displayed fading as if never there. His face hardened, and he brought the revolver up, pointing the barrel at my face. It remained there for a moment, the crowd quieting, watching intently now. Waiting for the show to begin.

"Which..." he said, shifting his aim to Neil's face.

"...one..." he said, taking aim at me again.

"...will..."

Back to Neil.

"...I..."

And to me again.

"...shoot..."

Neil.

"...to..."

Me. He held his aim for a moment, then finished his method of selection.

"...day?"

The long barreled .44 magnum revolver shifted from me once more and found its mark on my friend as Perkins grinned darkly and squeezed the trigger.

Click.

Neil never flinched as the hammer came down on an empty chamber.

"It's your lucky day," Perkins said. "For now."

He altered his aim to me and, without hesitation, squeezed the trigger again.

Click.

"Fortune smiles on you, Fletch," he said, then once more pointed the revolver at Neil.

Click.

"I was never a math whiz, but I's say your collective luck is about fifty percent used up," Perkins mocked us.

"Do it!"

The urging came from the crowd. From one person in the crowd—Sheryl Quincy. She was no longer a silent observer. The moment had come for her to take ownership of what was happening, and she was doing so without hesitation.

The mob, it appeared, was complete.

"Fletch," Perkins said, and pointed the revolver at me.

Click.

"Well, this just gets more interesting by the second," he said, swinging the weapon to Neil for the fifth pull of the trigger.

Click.

An audible gasp rippled through the crowd. Five trigger pulls on five empty chambers. Every single person knew what that meant. They waited, watching as Perkins shifted his aim to me again.

I stared at the man past the barrel of the revolver, one eye lined up with the weapon's blade sights. He smiled at me as his finger rubbed the trigger, up and down, a simple application of pressure all that was needed to end the game.

To end me.

Then, without warning or explanation, he pulled the large handgun away from me and placed the muzzle against his own temple. Someone in the crowd screamed 'No!' Perkins, though, did not heed their plea. Nor did he stop grinning at me as he pulled the trigger a final time.

Click.

The gasp from the crowd this time was different, a mix of horror and relief in it. Perkins lowered the revolver to his side again, still fixed on me.

"Oops," he said. "I guess I only had five bullets in it."

He began to chuckle. Slowly, those who followed him began to let their shock subside and laugh along with him. It seemed to me right then that he'd cultivated more than followers—they were worshipers.

Perkins slid the revolver into its holster angled across the front of his belt and let his gaze moved between Neil and me. He held a hand up to quiet the crowd, and when their burst of giddiness ended he spoke.

"Gentlemen, where is BA Four Twelve?"

Neil's head bowed a bit, as if he'd been posed this very question before, over and over again. I, too, wanted to ask him the very same thing. But not as it was being done now, by this man.

"One of you knows," Perkins said. "Maybe both of you know. But eventually, and by that I mean soon, at least one of you will give me what I want."

Biological Agent Four Eleven was the blight. Four Twelve was its cousin meant for the human population of planet earth. Tyler Olin, Neil's former CIA colleague, if the man was to be believed, had told the tale of my friend stealing a sample of the deadly pathogen so that the government would not be its only possessor. Somewhere along the way between that action and his leaving Bandon, the man next to me had, apparently, hidden that hideously valuable item for safekeeping.

There was no guarantee that 'safe' would hold any meaning in perpetuity. Not with someone like Perkins on the hunt for Four Twelve. In a movie I might have screamed out to the man that he was mad. But this wasn't a movie. It was all too real, and the reason he wanted it was no mystery to me.

"Even if we knew, and we told you, you couldn't use it to take Bandon," I said.

"And why is that, Fletch?" Perkins challenged me.

"It's persistent," I told him, recalling what Tyler Olin had shared about the deadly biological agent. "Once it kills, the virus will still be there. On the bodies. Maybe in the air. The only thing you accomplish by using it on Bandon is creating a ghost town."

"That's a scary story," Perkins said. "But it also sounds like a load of bull."

Behind him, Sheryl Quincy climbed onto the flatbed and approached, standing next to her man.

"He's lying," she said. "Weatherly never said anything like that about Four Twelve."

"This is the same Weatherly who led the Unified Government into annihilation?" I asked.

Quincy stepped forward and brought a hand hard across my face, leaving my cheek stinging. When I recovered, I looked her straight in the eye and spit a wad of blood drawn by the blow onto the truck bed at her feet. Sensing that she might react, Perkins put a hand up, stopping any further assault.

"We need them able to talk," Perkins said. "He can't very well do that with a mouthful of broken teeth."

Sheryl considered his order, delivered more gently to her than I suspected it would have been to any other. After a moment she drew her own mouthful of pure spit and let it fly at my feet before turning and hopping down from the flatbed. I watched her push fast through the crowd, disappearing in the darkness beyond the burning barrels.

"I could have just let her loose on you," Perkins told me. "You can ask your friend there how much fun that can be."

I turned toward Neil briefly. His bowed head angled toward me, and for the first time I noticed the remnants of old bruises, jaundiced patches on his jawline where he'd been struck repeatedly. And viciously.

They tried to beat it out of him...

"But Sheryl teaching you a lesson won't give me what I need," Perkins said. "Not on its own. See, I realize that you may know where it is, or you may not. You may have fed Weatherly a load of bull to drive him away from Bandon the first time, but Neil here, he most certainly knows where the virus is. And your presence allows me a new way forward."

The tyrant wanted the answer to Four Twelve. He wanted its location. And now he had both the man who could give it to him, and leverage to make that happen.

Me.

"Fletch, you are going to be instrumental in convincing our mutual friend here to be more forthcoming," Perkins said. "We can get started on that in a couple days. Before then, maybe you can convince him to open up. That would spare you from a great deal of unpleasantness."

The crowd chuckled at that word—unpleasantness. They knew, as did I, that it was a highly sanitized description of what I was facing. If Perkins couldn't get what he needed from my friend through the infliction of pain, he might be able to do so by doing the same to me. Or worse.

"It will be quite a show for my people, Fletch," Perkins said, and his followers erupted, applause and cheers rising. "With you as the star."

Perkins eyed me for a moment, smiling. He was in a position of power, and he knew it. But it wasn't ultimate power. If it was, I would be dead. As would Neil. We still had something to offer him, which was why we were alive. For now.

In a small way, which might seem inconsequential, we still held that power over him. Denying him what he desired would keep us alive. All that remained to be seen was how long Neil and I could manage to resist.

"Put them back in their cages," Perkins said.

Bryce and Jake climbed onto the flatbed and untied us from the metalwork at the rear of the cab, leaving our hands and arms bound like angel wings as they hauled us down from the truck. I glanced back toward Perkins as we were manhandled through the crowd. The man was almost giddy, joyously smiling from ear to ear.

Until he wasn't.

His expression turned harsh as the sound of the bell clanging rose. I looked toward it, and thought it seemed to be coming from atop the bank building we were being taken back to.

"Aircraft!"

Someone in the crowd shouted that, and things switched into some oddly non-chaotic quickened motion. Bryce and Jake picked up their pace, pulling Neil and me along, while behind us a half dozen people grabbed five-gallon buckets that had been pre-filled with water and poured them into the burning barrels. As the fires were quenched, others put lids atop the steel containers and flipped them over. Up and down the street, the few artificial lights that had been on went dark, and people ducked quickly inside the blacked-out buildings.

By the time Neil and I were hustled back into the bank, the world outside was swallowed by night, dark and silent.

A few minutes later, the plane came.

Three

We were locked back in our cells, our hands and arms unbound, as the aircraft buzzed the town at low altitude.

"You're wondering," Neil said.

"A lot of things," I confirmed.

I sat against the wall of my cell, close to the bars, straining to see out of the vault to where Jake stood guard, his warming fire doused with every other source of light in town.

"They have scouts two miles out," Neil told me. "Eight of them. One every forty-five degrees. If they hear or see anything they send a signal on their radios. No words, just clicks on the mic. Three for intruders on land, four for aircraft. A sentry in town rings the bell if it's aircraft. Otherwise the warning is passed by word of mouth."

"That's comprehensive," I said.

"I've had a couple years to absorb their tactics," Neil said. "Their procedures."

I looked away from the vault's opening to my friend. In the near total darkness I could only make out the faintest features of him as he lay on the floor near the bars, head resting on one thin arm like some bony pillow.

"He doesn't think they're ready," Neil said, his gaze angling upward as the aircraft made another low pass over the town. "They need time to prepare before making their move on Bandon. That's why hiding is an art form for his people. Perkins has them drill getting to cover constantly."

"This isn't a drill," I said.

"No," Neil confirmed. "It's not. Is the plane from Bandon?"

"No," I said.

That answer brought with it new questions. I knew that Chris Beekman could not have both reached the abandoned aircraft he'd spotted and made one of them airworthy already. Even if he had, which was impossible, that he could have received word from Bandon on our location was even less likely. The calls that Dave Arndt and I had put out announcing our intention to land near Klamath Falls hadn't been acknowledged.

Yet there was a plane overhead, a single-engine aircraft by the sound of it. It had come from somewhere, and carried at least one person. One person who was very interested in the dead town below.

"Do they get many air warnings?" I asked.

Across from me, Neil eased himself up and shook his head as he sat resting near the bars.

"This is the first," he answered.

That bit of information only added to the oddness of the event. The oddness of everything.

"Neil, listen..."

"Soon all that drama Perkins went through won't be for show," he said, ignoring my request. "The gun won't be unloaded."

"Neil..."

"They'll kill us, but first they're going to hurt you, Fletch," he went on. "Probably worse than they hurt me. And they hurt me in ways that..."

He stopped there, abandoning that thread of explanation and looking to me.

"Fletch, tell me about Grace. And Krista. And..."

He began to choke up as he tried to utter the name of his son. The child he'd hardly had any chance to know before Grace and their children were sent back to Bandon as Neil remained with the Unified Government forces.

"Brandon is terrific," I said. "Grace and Krista, too."

He smiled through the threat of tears, his gaze thick behind the puddled emotion. It was a burst of happy relief he was showing, but would it remain as such if I continued? If I told him more of those he cherished. More about Grace and the life she'd lived when it was believed he was dead.

I would not share that. Not yet.

"Neil, I need some answers," I said, and my friend nodded slowly, a few errant tears finally spilling.

"I would think you do," he said as he wiped his cheeks. "You said you saw me die."

"Yes," I confirmed. "Tyler Olin shot you."

Neil snickered, a quiet flourish of gallows humor as he shook his head. "Ty Olin."

"He slipped into Bandon during the Unified Government siege," I explained. "He said your Ranger signal was some sort of warning."

Neil stared at me for a few seconds, saying nothing, adding what I'd said to some collection data points that seemed to be building some understanding within.

"I imagine he told you all about me," Neil said, eyeing me through the din. "About who I really was."

"Central Intelligence Agency," I said. "You're a spy."

"I was," he corrected me. "Now I'm just...I'm this."

He gestured weakly to the gaunt frame that defined his physicality.

"Yeah. But you're alive, and I don't understand how that's possible."

Neil glanced briefly through the vault door, to where Jake stood near the front of the bank, peering out its shattered windows as the sound of the aircraft began to recede. The man was out of earshot, and that seemed to be what concerned my friend—privacy. What he was about to share with me he wanted no one else to know.

"You didn't see me die, Fletch," he said as he looked back to me. "You saw a man named Riley Grimes die."

I didn't question his statement. I simply waited for some further explanation which would make what he'd just shared believable.

"If you lived in the world that I did, and you did the things that I did, certain things were extremely helpful," he told me. "It was a benefit to be seen in one location, doing a completely ordinary thing, while also working half a world away gathering intelligence on a drug cartel's links to Philippine terrorists."

It took me a moment to process not just what he had said, but what it suggested.

"A double," I said.

"He was paid handsomely to fill in for me in the mundane things that Neil Moore the mid-level diplomat might do," my friend explained. "Take my place at social events. Personal appointments."

The way my friend looked at me after those last words hinted at something he was both embarrassed by, and proud of.

"What do you mean 'personal'?"

"Remember the Seahawks game we went to?" Neil asked.

I did. It was several years before the blight appeared. A boy's weekend trip to Seattle to take in a football game, which we had.

Or, which *I* had.

"That was him?"

Neil nodded. I shook my head.

"I spent forty-eight hours with..."

I couldn't finish the statement. Neil could sense the sudden doubt rising within me.

"That was his job, Fletch. He'd been briefed on every aspect of my life so he could slip into it when that was required. It wasn't done to fool you, it was done—"

"To protect you," I said, finishing the explanation for him. "I get that. It's just that...to me that was you. We talked about things going back decades."

And we had, comparing the game we were watching to our own exploits on the field in high school. There was no way then that I would have known that the person I was sitting next to was not the friend I'd grown up with. Even now that possibility bordered on the unbelievable.

But it made sense. All that he was telling me did. Except for one thing.

"That was all before, Neil. How did this Grimes guy end up getting shot down by Olin?"

"When things started falling apart, Riley made a choice," my friend said. "As the Unified Government rose and ours fell, he sought out Weatherly. By that time the good general had shifted his own loyalty. He was the real deal to Riley. Once they hooked up, Weatherly had all the information he needed about me. He had his spies inside our military reach out when we were in Skagway."

"You told me that when you left Bandon," I reminded him.

Marines had come in on Ospreys to evacuate some of the survivors in the ungainly tilt-rotor aircraft. As had some covert liaison from the Unified Government.

"Black is white," Neil said, repeating the mantra he'd shared in those last moments we'd shared before leaving with Grace and Krista.

"And white is black," I said, completing the statement for him. "Were you talking about your double when you said that?"

"I wasn't sure," Neil said. "But I was worried. To have Weatherly send people to me, trying to get me to switch sides, I knew he had to have more information than just my dual life. He was deeply enmeshed in military and intelligence before the blight, so he could have known about me. But after Skagway, I was afraid there were more turncoats already in place."

"There was," I said.

"You said something about me being traded for Sheryl Quincy," Neil said.

It was becoming clear to me that much of what I'd seen my friend do, or say, had not been him at all.

"Weatherly paraded you on camera," I said. "Over an amateur TV transmission. You were bruised. He said you were going to be executed for betraying him."

"That wasn't me," Neil said, drawing a long breath that ended in a shallow, wet cough. "Weatherly played his hand there to get his spy back. He knew you'd do anything to save me."

I nodded. But I wasn't pleased with myself for understanding that. It was quite the opposite, in fact.

"And all I did was invite your double into Bandon," I said.

"It sounds like Ty Olin took care of that for you," Neil observed.

"He wanted to kill you," I told my friend.

"I know," Neil said, quieting for a moment before going on. "That wasn't me putting out the Ranger call."

"I get that now."

"Weatherly was only afraid of one thing," Neil said.

"Four Twelve," I replied.

Neil nodded and pulled his frail body closer to the bars.

"He knew that Ty and I worked together to get samples of that and Four Eleven," Neil explained. "When I wasn't being forthcoming with my answers, he had Grimes record the Ranger warning."

"That was a long shot," I said. "That Olin would even be alive, that he'd be close enough to receive the transmission."

Now my friend shook his head, dismissing my downward quantification of his old partner's drive and ability.

"Having met Olin, you should understand that's not even close to being accurate," Neil said.

I stared at him for a moment. There was truth to what he was saying, I realized. But there was another truth as well—Tyler Olin had underestimated me.

"I killed Olin," I said.

Neil straightened a bit where he sat, absorbing what I'd just told him.

"I killed him because he killed you," I said. "Except he didn't."

"He would have," Neil said. "He didn't have any idea Grimes would be where he was. My guess is Ty thought I would have done what we were supposed to do."

"Which is?"

"Eliminate our double if there was a likelihood of compromise."

"So he had one, too," I said.

"He was probably worm food before he knew what was happening," Neil said.

He quieted for a moment. We both did. There was no more sound of any aircraft. That silence that the blight had brought upon the devastated world settled over us, and all that surrounded us. I'd almost forgotten what it was like. Bandon had left that foul hush behind. People laughed. Birds chirped.

Here, though, the world was still as it had been. There was no recovery. Even the green that had drawn Dave Arndt and I down to investigate was faux, just bait for the trap that had taken his life and left me captive.

"They killed Dave," I said, nodding toward the vault door.

"Dave Arndt?"

I confirmed Neil's question with a nod. He'd known the man during his time in Bandon.

"Perkins will kill anything that gets in his way."

"That's not a surprise," I said.

"If he gets to Bandon..."

He didn't finish the grim suggestion, letting the truncated worry hand for a moment before he shifted to a subject I knew he would choose to revisit.

"You said Grace and the kids are okay," Neil said.

"They are."

"How is she holding up?" he asked. "From what you said, she had to think I died. She had no idea about Riley Grimes. I never shared that with her."

"It was hard on her, Neil," I said, being as honest as I could while telling him nothing of what I knew I would have to.

He accepted my words, but puzzled at them. At the manner in which I'd delivered them—with apology dripping from the few syllables.

"Fletch..."

I didn't look away from my friend. I wouldn't. Not with what I would have to share. Words that I knew would hurt.

"Neil, she moved on."

He let that hang there for a moment, understanding the reality which spun from the comment. Still, he wanted more. He wanted to know.

And he deserved nothing less than that.

"She remarried, Neil. They have a child. A little girl named Alice. Brandon and Krista adore her."

There was almost no light that reached us in the depths of the bank vault. But enough trickled in from the starry night beyond the open front of the building that I could see the sheen of tears build over my friend's eyes. The pain he was feeling I could not imagine, having lost his family through distance and captivity, only to learn that it was worse than that.

"I'm sorry," I said.

His gaze drifted about for a moment and his hands reached to the bars, fingers flexing tight around the thick lengths of steel, squeezing with a force I could not only imagine, but that I could see. For all the wasting which had afflicted his body, his hands had remained surprisingly strong, I now noticed.

"Who did she marry?" Neil asked.

"You don't know him."

"Who?" he repeated.

"His name's Clay Genesee. He's a doctor. He was Navy when he came in with support elements to help sustain Bandon."

"He was military?"

I nodded.

"And he came in? Like Sheryl Quincy came in?"

I knew where he was going with the question. With the suggestion, really. I had to cut that off, if for no other reason than to end any hope on his part that there was some scenario that would remove Clay and put himself back in Grace's life.

"He's not like that, Neil. He's a good man."

His stare hardened. At me in particular. I wasn't taking sides because there were no sides to take. Circumstances, a grossly unfair collection of them, had crafted the reality he now faced. Nothing more.

"I guess Grimes was convincing to the end," Neil said.

"I thought it was you," I told him. "If I didn't know, how could she? How could anyone?"

His gaze drifted off, settling on a point lost in the darkness at the back of his cell. Then, without a word, he slid his withered body away from the bars until he was lost in the shadows.

"Neil..."

My friend didn't answer. Not then, nor when I called to him time after time over the following minutes. It was as if, once again, he was gone from my life.

Four

I woke to weak morning light spilling into my cell and the tap of metal against the bars.

"Rise and shine..."

My eyes opened from the exhausted sleep to see Perkins clicking the barrel of his revolver between the bars, Bryce and Jake behind him. Past them the new day had brightened the bank beyond the vault.

"Time to get started on your cooperation, Fletch," Perkins said, smiling.

I glanced past the men and saw Neil crawling slowly toward the bars from the back of his cell, his gaze shifting between our captors and me. The anger and hurt which my news had brought over him was gone, replaced by a different pairing of emotions.

Fear and concern.

"On your feet," Bryce said as Perkins stepped back from my cell door.

I did as was ordered, knowing that Bryce's pump shotty, or Jake's double barrel, or their leader's .44 magnum monster could easily end Neil and me in seconds. It was still not time to resist, despite what I believed we were about to face.

In one very small, yet incredibly important way, I was wrong.

"We'll have him back in a bit," Perkins said, looking to my still-caged friend after I'd been trussed up and stood outside my cell.

Neil pulled himself up with his surprisingly strong hands until he stood, supported by the bars. The fear that I'd seen rise in him had a semblance of an explanation now—confusion. What he was witnessing right now was not just unexplained—it was unexpected.

"What are you doing?" Neil asked, demanding a response from Perkins directly.

The man turned toward my friend, eyeing him for a few seconds before whipping the long barrel of his revolver at his fingers. Neil quickly withdrew his hands, leaving the weapon to smack hard against the thick metal, saving his fingers. His grip released, he slid to the floor against the wall.

"That's right," Perkins said to him. "Cower like the coward you are."

He turned and nodded toward the exit and Bryce pulled me out of the vault. I managed to glance back just once before I could no more, and saw Neil once again standing as Perkins and Jake followed us out. His hands were wrapped around the bars once more, supporting his weakened body, and his gaze was locked with mine. It wasn't the sort of exchange that people shared when one would never see the other again.

But it wasn't far from that.

* * *

There was no flatbed truck this time, just an old pickup that reminded me of my own back at home.

Home...

Elaine would be worried. Beyond that, I knew. It was certain that we were considered missing by this point. Efforts would be underway to determine what had happened and where we were.

That 'we' would be Dave Arndt and me—not Neil Moore. But it mattered not who I was with. Bandon would be arranging some sort of search in the vicinity of our last known positions. Camas Valley and Remote would lend assistance.

But distance would make any effort difficult. Chris Beekman, once he had a working aircraft, would spearhead the search, I was certain. We were the needle in a very big haystack that he would be charged with finding.

That, though, could be days away. Weeks, maybe, if the planes he'd gone to salvage required extensive repair. For now, we were on our own. And, for the moment, I was on *my* own.

"Just tell him," Bryce said.

He rode with me in the back of the pickup, resting against the rear of the cab while I was secured to the tailgate. Perkins drove, which surprised me. I'd thought a bevy of servants and acolytes would be at his beck and call to perform menial tasks such as chauffeuring him from place to place. Perhaps, though, in Bryce's suggestion there was a hint of some explanation.

Perkins was all about power. To have those outside his inner circle be witness to one who continued to defy him might be detrimental to the image of a strong leader he'd constructed. More than strong, actually—beyond resisting. How many had stood up to him and lived to tell the tale? So far just Neil. And now me.

"Why?" I pressed Bryce as the pickup turned off the main road and followed streets through the deathly stillness of a neighborhood savaged long ago by the blight.

"It would just be best that you do," Bryce said.

I found it immediately odd. The way he'd responded to my challenge was not some harsh rhetoric meant to bolster his leader's intentions. Instead it seemed simply a statement tinged with...humanity? How that was possible, I did not know.

But I was about to find out.

The pickup pulled into the parking lot of the town's high school and stopped next to the gymnasium, one wall largely broken out, mounds of charred rubble piled at the base of the penetration. Wrecked cars littered the lot, and as I was pulled from the back of the pickup by Perkins and Bryce and hauled toward the gym, I glanced into one of the vehicles, its rusting shell resting on four flat tires. In the front seat a decomposed body rested in a seat which had partly dissolved under the rotting flesh. What remained was mostly mummified, stretched skin torn in spots by bones protruding through it.

It had been a long time since I'd seen a direct victim of the blight. But I was far from Bandon. Far from the town and its surrounding hamlets which had been cleansed of such reminders of what had been so common at one time. Bodies. The anonymous dead everywhere. Glimpsing what I had, I realized that they were still everywhere. The world was mostly still dead. A funeral pyre in waiting.

That resurfaced knowledge made me, once again, think of home. Of Elaine. Of our daughter, Hope. I hadn't even told Neil about her. I sincerely hoped that I would get that chance.

"Inside," Perkins said as we reached a side door to the gymnasium.

He held it open and Bryce manhandled me through. The space was surprisingly bright, daylight pouring through the large hole in the partially collapsed wall, enough that I could plainly see the devastated interior. Wooden bleachers had been stripped, and a collection of lights and ceiling fixtures which had once hung above were scattered about, time and weather having weakened their mounts.

I also saw Sheryl Quincy, standing at the center of the warped wood floor, a person tied to a chair next to her, white hood draped over their head. It was a man, I thought, and his body trembled, quiet sobs rattling through him.

"Keep moving," Perkins ordered.

I did, my pace slowing some as we neared those who were waiting for us. For me. Bryce nudged me with his shotgun, an almost gentle push this time, no jarring thump to my back. Was that some sudden humanity rising again? I doubted it.

Perkins grabbed my trussed arms where they were lashed behind my head and guided me to a place facing the bound man. He was not tied as I was, his hands behind his back and cinched tightly to the chair, his ankles secured to each front leg.

"Go ahead," Perkins said.

At his command, Sheryl reached to the man and snatched the hood from his head. He was maybe fifty, with a salt and pepper beard and hair that was stringy and too long. There was that distantly familiar thinness about him. He was one of those countless people I'd seen over the years who had just survived, barely, their body always on the precipice of starvation.

"Fletch, I'd like to introduce you to..." Perkins paused, looking to the man. "Tell him your name."

The man hesitated, his wide, terrified gaze moving between Perkins and me.

"Go ahead," Perkins urged him gently. "Fletch here is your new best friend."

Finally the man fixed his wet, reddened gaze on me.

"I'm Fr...Frank Wallace."

"Frank, meet Fletch," Perkins said, nodding to Bryce as he stepped away, the guard taking hold of me now. "You two are now fast friends. Do you know how I know that?"

I kept my eye on Perkins as he took a position next to Frank Wallace. On the other side, Sheryl stood, flanking him. But only for a moment until she very purposely stepped away from that spot.

No...

She was now out of the line of fire.

"Fletch, do you remember that game we played last night?" Perkins asked, drawing his revolver from its holster.

Frank Wallace turned to see the man produce the weapon, his already terrified gaze swelling. His gaze shifted back to me, as if I could provide some explanation of what was happening. Or was about to happen.

"Perkins," I said. "Don't."

He opened the weapon's cylinder and dumped six rounds into his palm, pocketing five and very obviously holding one for all to see.

"This time, Fletch, we're playing for keeps," Perkins said, inserting the single round into the cylinder and snapping it shut. "Not just playing."

Without any warning he brought the weapon up and leveled the barrel at the captive's head. Frank tried to lean away, head pulled toward his shoulders as he cowered.

"Fletch, where is Four Twelve?" Perkins asked.

"Earl," I said, making an attempt at some human connection with the man. "This is not the way to—"

He pulled the trigger and a terrifying *CLICK* sounded. Frank screamed, his whole body shaking violently as he looked to me, his gaze pleading.

"What is happening?" he begged. "Stop him! Please!"

"Fletch," Perkins prompted me.

"Dammit, I don't know!" I shouted at him.

CLICK.

"Noooooo!" Frank screamed. "No! Please!"

"Ask your friend to be forthright," Perkins told the man.

Frank focused on me, leaning forward against his bindings.

"Please, just give him what he wants. Whatever he wants. Please."

"What's it going to be, Fletch?" Perkins asked.

I tried to move, wanting instinctively to charge the murderous dictator, but Bryce's hold on me was unbreakable.

"So, no answer still?"

"I don't—"

CLICK.

"Ahhhhhhh!" Frank Wallace screamed. "Dear God, what's happening?!"

I looked away from the man who'd been brought here to motivate me. To gain my compliance. I couldn't bear the look of terror he was laying upon me anymore. Instead I gave my full attention to Perkins.

"He's not part of this," I said. "This isn't about him."

"Four Twelve, Fletch?" Perkins asked again.

I had no answer for him, so I gave none. He pulled the trigger again. This time there was no click.

The single round fired, exploding from the barrel and tearing through Frank Wallace's head, from left to right, ripping half the man's skull away as the horrific blast of blood and brain matter sprayed halfway across the gym floor. His body and the chair it was bound to toppled from the force of the impact and came to rest in a spreading pool of the man's blood.

I turned my head, looking away as Perkins took a fresh round from his pocket and added it to the five he'd removed, reloading the weapon fully before holstering it. He stepped toward me and grabbed my chin, forcing me to look him in the eye.

"Plenty more where he came from, Fletch," Perkins said, his breath foul and warm on my face. "You're going to answer me. Soon. Because eventually the body count will include you or your friend."

He released my chin and stepped back, eyeing the horror he'd created.

"Who was he?"

The question rose without any intent. Something within me simply sought some context as to why Frank Wallace had been chosen to suffer this fate. And who, among the many Perkins had mentioned, was he?

It wasn't Perkins who answered, though.

"Some slob survivor," Sheryl said. "Someone who should have been dead long ago but didn't know enough to let it happen."

Perkins smiled and nodded at his companion's harsh critique.

"You see why I like her?" Perkins said. "He's a nobody, Fletch. Just a poor bastard who wandered into town. Not one of us, but he wanted our spoils. All we'd worked for."

"In other words he wanted help," I said.

Perkins chuckled.

"Fletch, you of all people should know that nothing in this world gets handed to you anymore. It has to be fought for. It has to be won."

"To the victor goes *everything*," Sheryl said, referencing a spin on her leader's 'spoils' comment.

It was becoming abundantly clear that I was facing something new. Neil had been dealing with it already. The machinations of Perkins and his kind were a given by now to him. Not to me. The depravity, the drive, that the man exhibited and possessed were not what he saw as necessary evils. They were just part of who he was.

"Fletch, you're an honorable guy," Perkins said. "Naivete doesn't negate that completely. And in that trait I'd found your weakness. Both you and Neil. You see, I realized last night when neither of you spoke up to save the other that your sense of honor to one another won't allow you to break. But I imagine that the next time you face what just transpired here, your resolve will begin to crack. And who knows, maybe the right person in that chair will break you altogether. Another man. A woman. A child."

Dear God...

"I don't know," I said. "I don't have the answer you want."

Perkins smiled and nodded.

"Keep telling yourself that, Fletch," he said.

He turned and walked away from me, taking Sheryl's hand as they left the gymnasium.

"I told you to tell him," Bryce said.

Then he twisted me harshly around and aimed me at the exit, leaving the horror he'd been party to behind.

Five

I was driven back to the bank and returned to my cell. Opposite me, once we were alone, Neil spoke.

"What did they do?"

"Nothing to me," I said.

My tone expressed that he shouldn't press for more details. Not now. And he didn't. He knew me, as I knew him. Or as I thought I had.

"How did you do it, Neil?" I asked. "How did you keep everything from me?"

"Don't you mean 'why'?"

I supposed his correction was more accurate than what I'd asked.

"Okay...why?"

"Because that was my job," he answered, providing the simplest, most obvious response. "And I was good at it. And I believed that what I was doing was important. So with all that in mind, just understand that me hiding what I did from you was to protect me, and to protect you. I wanted to keep doing what I was meant to do, being who I was meant to be, but I couldn't manage that if either of us was compromised."

"I wasn't the spy, Neil."

"You were the spy's best friend," he said. "That was enough. People who suspected the truth about me, or knew it outright, are always aware of who men like me are close to."

As he explained his rationale, I could understand. The lack of further details did not diminish my acceptance. Mostly, though, I trusted my friend.

My friend...

"Elaine and I got married," I said. "A while after you left with Grace and Krista."

"She's the right woman for you," Neil told me. "It only took the end of the world to bring you two together."

I allowed a soft chuckle. It was true what he said. Before Elaine I'd rarely even thought about 'settling down'. I was all about my business, and my freedom. But with her, through her, I found more freedom than I'd ever expected to know. And more joy.

"We have a daughter," I said. "We named her Hope."

I continued, filling him in on all that had transpired in Bandon, and with its residents, since his disappearance and supposed death. He took it all in without reacting, showing no emotion until I was finished. Then he spoke, a sadness about him.

"I'm sorry about Elaine," he said. "It shouldn't have been her getting hurt. I should have been there with you. It should have been me."

"She's all right," I assured my friend. "If there was still a Daytona Five Hundred I think she could place top ten in that chair of hers."

He accepted my words, even smiling lightly after a moment.

"Hope, eh?"

I nodded.

"You named her," I said.

"There's always hope," Neil said, repeating the mantra he'd shared first when warning me about the coming blight. "I want to believe that."

He shifted his attention from me to the space beyond the vault. Jake had his small warming fire burning again, something sizzling in a pan over it.

"He's making us lunch," Neil told me, his voice kept low.

"You need to eat," I said.

"I might eat later," Neil said.

"I'm just...worried about you," I shared.

Neil fixed his gaze hard on our guard in the ransacked front of the bank building. It was not an angry stare. It was more...focused. I'd seen it before in him, as far back as high school, when he was sizing up an opponent on the thirty-yard line before the snap.

"Things are going to get bad, Fletch," he said.

"I know."

He looked to me now, that same intensity in his eyes. I could feel it across the six feet that separated our cells.

"It's going to be okay," he told me. "Trust me."

"There's always hope?" I suggested.

He shook his head slowly and laced the fingers of both hands together, squeezing hard. Enough so that his knuckles cracked with sharp, almost painful snaps.

"We don't need hope," he said. "Because I have a plan."

"Lunchtime," Jake said as he came into the vault, two small cups in hand. "Some sort of chicken thing from an old MRE."

He crouched and placed the cups just outside our cells and stepped back. I reached through the bars, only managing to get a flattened hand out before the meat of my wrist prevented any further reach. I pinched the edge of the container between two fingers and slid it into my cell.

"It's good food, Neil," Jake said, looking to my sickly friend. "I had some already. Tastes like real chicken. It's got some peas in there, too. Gravy's not bad, either."

Neil slid back from the bars into the shadows of his cell, curling up in the back corner.

"Maybe I'll have some dinner later," my friend said.

Jake nodded. He seemed to actually be a bit concerned with one of his prisoner's condition and looked to me as I smelled the contents of the cup.

"I'll leave his cup," Jake said. "See if you can get him to eat. He doesn't hardly eat anything."

The man left us. I tipped the cup and sampled some of the chicken mixture before chewing and swallowing more of it.

"Neil," I said.

Looking across the space between us, I could just make out his position shifting as he looked toward me.

"What plan?" I asked.

"Later," he said.

Then he turned away again and said no more, settling into a deep sleep, wet coughs bursting every so often. There was reason to worry about him, I knew. Anyone who'd laid eyes on him could see he was in trouble physically.

And yet, he spoke of some plan. But a plan to what? Escape seemed unlikely with the realities of our captivity. The cell bars were unbeatable I knew from some simple testing I'd done. The lock, similarly, that secured the chain around the door was not pickable. Not by me, at least.

'Because I have a plan...'

I had to trust that what my friend had said was true, whatever it meant. And whatever it meant for us.

Six

Night came, and so did Perkins.

He was accompanied by no one. Neither Bryce nor Sheryl were with him, and Jake remained in the front of the bank as the colony's leader came to our cells.

"Jake's cooking you up a special dinner," Perkins said.

I'd noticed the scent drifting back from the guard's small cooking area near his fire. The terrible, familiar smell.

"A nice big helping of Frank Wallace," the man said, reaching down to pat a spot on his pants below his front pocket. "Thigh, I believe. Should be fairly tender."

"Not gonna happen, Perkins," I said.

The man sniffed a laugh and looked into Neil's cell. My friend still slept there, breathing fitfully.

"I don't know," Perkins said. "Your buddy here looks like he could use a good meal."

He didn't know. If he had, if Neil had revealed what he'd had to do on our journey back from Cheyenne to stay alive, Perkins would be hammering us both with that. Whatever they'd tried, or managed to beat out of him, that morsel of information from our collective past hadn't been revealed.

"Is this it, Perkins?" I asked. "You make me watch someone die, then serve them up for dinner?"

"More than that," the man said. "I hope you enjoyed that chicken slop for lunch, because that's the last taste you're going to have of something not of your species until I get what I want."

He looked to Neil again, briefly, then focused back on me.

"When your friend wakes up, share the good news with him," Perkins said.

He flashed a smile at me, then left, giving Jake a quick thump on the shoulder as he passed, the guard tossing a salute that his leader ignored as he left the bank building.

"When Jake comes back, get him to face you," Neil said softly.

I looked to my friend. He'd rolled over and now faced the bars, still curled into an almost fetal position. I moved closer to the bars to hear his quiet words better.

"What are you talking about?"

"Fletch, just do it," Neil urged me. "Because pretty soon it's going to be one of us that Jake's frying up out there. You know that Perkins will take this thing all the way there."

I hadn't considered that, but my friend was right. In the twisted dictator's mind, he would see that as the ultimate card to play against us.

"Just do it, Fletch," Neil said. "Trust me."

I nodded, and he closed his eyes. If this was part of the plan he'd mentioned, I didn't know. But it seemed likely. We were fast approaching a decision point where the worst option was no option at all. Except Neil seemed to have, at least in his own mind, discovered another way.

* * *

A few minutes after Perkins left the bank, as I watched Jake filling two small cups with strips of seared, nauseating human flesh, a sound began to rise.

Cheering.

It was distant, but not too far. Maybe down the street a bit. Many voices blended together, with howls of approval and raucous clapping. I had little time to try to comprehend what it might be as our guard approached with our intended dinner.

"Mr. Perkins wants you two to eat this," he said, almost embarrassed, wincing slightly at the offering he had brought us.

He placed the two cups on the floor near our cells, just as he had done so when serving us lunch. As he began to back away toward the vault's exit, I stood and approached the bars.

"Jake..."

"What is it?"

'*...get him to face you...*'

What did Neil have up his sleeve? Some weapon hidden in his cell? That was impossible. There were no spaces to keep some makeshift knife or other implement out of view.

"I need to talk to you," I said.

Jake didn't approach, keeping his distance from the cells.

"About what?"

'*...get him to face you...*'

I had to trust my friend. I had to make it happen.

"I can't eat this," I said. "I can't."

"That's not...I have no say in this," Jake said.

"Listen, Jake, I just can't," I said. "I'll cooperate."

The man guarding us seemed genuinely surprised at what I'd said. He approached slowly, positioning himself in the space between the cells, standing midway between each. Even if I'd been able to squeeze my arms between the bars, he was still out of reach. But I was not doing this for that purpose—I was playing this charade because my friend wanted me to.

"You want me to get Perkins?" Jake asked, suddenly self-conscious. "Mr. Perkins."

Before I could respond I saw something, though I forced myself not to react as I glimpsed Neil rise up in his cell directly behind Jake. His chiseled hands gripped the bars, but once he was upright they slipped through the space between, as did his wrists, forearms, and elbows, until the length of both withered arms were stretched out toward our guard.

You son of a...

I didn't mentally complete the term of both surprise and admiration as I came instantly to understand the ingeniousness and fortitude that my friend possessed. He'd done this. Prepared for this, though not *exactly* this. He would have had no idea that we would be reunited in captivity. Instead, he'd subjected himself to starvation so that when the opportunity arose, a confluence of circumstance and timing, he could act.

He could strike.

For the briefest instant, past Jake, I caught Neil's eye, and I knew what he needed me to do beyond luring Jake close—but not close enough.

"I could just tell you, Jake," I said.

Then, as the mildly feeble man considered what I'd said, I made my move, lunging at the bars I could not get through. That did not matter. His reaction was instinctive. He recoiled, taking a quick step back, away from me.

And into Neil's grasp.

My friend had denied himself food for some time now, it was obvious, so that he could thin his arms enough to fit them between the bars that confined him. But, while he'd neglected his body, he focused what strength he retained on one thing—his hands. As I'd noticed, they remained strong. Powerful, even. What exercises he'd managed in private to maintain them I did not know, but when Jake was close enough Neil seized him, hands grasping the surprised man's head, fingers hooking into his eye sockets with terrible pressure as my friend jerked him backward against the bars.

Jake's head smashed against the solid steel with a sickly crack, his body going limp, cups of our intended meal tumbling to the floor. As he slid downward, Neil maintained his hold, and smashed the back of the man's skull against the bars again and again until, even in the dim light from the fire beyond the vault, I could see the wet red pool building beneath him on the concrete floor.

Neil, though, wasn't satisfied. He reached around Jake's neck and put one forearm in place, drawing it hard against the windpipe, choking whatever life remained from the motionless man.

"He's dead, Neil," I said.

My friend, though, didn't let go. He kept the pressure up.

"Neil..."

Finally, when he was satisfied that he'd sent our guard to his maker, he released him. Jake's upper body tipped to the right and Neil was left with his arms hanging outside the bars, spent.

"He has keys," my friend said through nearly gasping breaths.

"Can you get them?"

Neil nodded and repositioned his arms through the lower section of the bars, slipping one hand into Jake's left pocket. They emerged with a small ring, two keys on it.

"You've been planning for this," I said.

"For something like this," he partly corrected me.

He gripped the bars and hauled himself upward so that he could reach the upper section where the chain and lock secured the barred door. But the violent act he'd just completed had sapped whatever strength he'd held in reserve, and he collapsed back to the floor, sitting awkwardly, one arm propping his body up like a kickstand.

"Fletch," he said, the hand that didn't hold him up reaching toward the bars, the key ring in it.

"I've got it, buddy," I said.

He managed to get his hand through and slide the ring across the space between the cells. I retrieved it and unlocked my cell, then moved quickly to his, opening the door and reaching my friend.

"I'll get you up,' I said, crouching to get an arm under him.

"We've got maybe ten minutes before the show finishes," he said.

I lifted him and helped him from the cell. We made our way out of the vault and to where Jake's cooking fire still burned.

"What show?" I asked.

"Perkins puts on this rousing rally thing once a week," Neil told me. "It would make Goebbels proud."

That explained the cheering and applause, I now knew.

"People will be in the streets as soon as it's over," Neil said as I lowered him to the chair Jake had occupied. "We need to—"

He paused, his gaze fixing on the small cooking grate above the fire, strips of meat charring upon it. Flesh that allowed terrible memories to come flooding back. With a fast kick my friend sent the grate and its contents tumbling.

"His shotgun," Neil said, nodding toward an old desk once he calmed.

I looked and saw the weapon, a small pouch of shells next to it. Nearby, stabbed into a wooden tabletop, was a knife. I retrieved it and the more potent weapon.

"Any idea where we should go?" I asked.

"Anywhere but here," Neil said.

"What about sentries?"

"I won't be much help against those," Neil said. "So let's not run into any."

"Simple as that, huh?"

"You know it," he said, the joking moment a welcome interlude.

But it couldn't last. I had to get the both of us out of there. It was clear that I'd be doing the heavy lifting for the moment, but I needed my friend to get some of his strength back as quickly as possible.

"Here," I said, snagging an open MRE pouch from near Jake's fire. "Shove whatever's in there in your pockets."

Neil did just that, breaking open a packet of stale crackers and feeding the contents into his mouth as I helped him up.

"There has to be a back exit," I said.

"There is," Neil confirmed. "Perkins has a nice little spot across the alley where he tied me to a chair to make it a fair fight and did some work on my ribs and my jaw."

A torture chamber of sorts. That was what my friend was telling me.

"I'd be all for sticking around to do some damage to our friend Earl," I said. "Except I want to get..."

I couldn't say what I wanted to. What was natural to say. Because, for Neil, I realized in that instant that the home he'd left was not the one he'd be returning to. If we made it out of there.

"Let's go home, Fletch," he said, speaking the word which I could not. "Let's go."

Part Two

Flight

Seven

I opened the back door as Neil leaned against the wall just inside the bank building's rear exit and cautiously looked outside. Across the narrow passage between structures was another door, likely to the den of pain Neil had mentioned. To the left the alley continued into darkness, and to the right it spilled into the street less than twenty feet in the distance.

"The show's still going," Neil said.

I nodded. The sound of applause was more pronounced with my head poked outside, and was coming from the left.

"Wherever it is it backs up to this alley," I said.

Neil nodded toward the door he'd been taken through before.

"It won't be locked," he said. "We can cross through to the next street."

"All right," I said.

I lent my friend a hand again, the double barrel shotgun slung over my right shoulder and knife tucked in my low boot. We crossed the narrow gap between the buildings and, as Neil had suggested, the door was not locked. He twisted the handle with his strong grip and we were inside.

If the bank had been dim, this was blind midnight, hardly a wisp of ambient moonlight trickling in. Ahead, though, past the vague outlines of a wooden chair bolted to the concrete floor, I could just make out the glint of broken glass. It had to be the shattered window of whatever this establishment had been in the old world.

"There'll be one sentry behind us on the roof of the bank," Neil said as I helped him toward the front of the old store. "And another one a few hundred yards due west of us."

"No one else?" I asked.

"Nobody skips the rallies," he assured me. "Mothers take their infants."

We just had to avoid being spotted by those charged with being lookouts. Neil, it seemed, had made a habit of gathering intelligence on the machinations of Perkins' colony and its inhabitants. No doubt aided by abilities honed during his secretive former life, he had obviously been planning for the very escape we'd carried out—only without me in attendance. He'd fixed where threats would be. Guards. Groups of survivors. Sentries. All to make his breakout and flight from captivity...

Wait...

That word which had rattled off in my thoughts took on sudden extra importance.

Flight...

It could mean 'to run', which had been its intended usage in my head. But it also meant something else.

"Can you still fly?" I asked my friend as we neared the front of the trashed old store.

"A plane?" he reacted, surprised at the question.

But only for a moment.

"You came in on a plane," he said.

"Perkins' and his people have it," I said. "We landed on a road just west of the river."

We paused near the front door of the business which I could now tell, from remnants of lettering on its broken windows, that it had been a liquor store. Neil looked to me, a hint of some energy rising in him.

"He'll have it at the airport by now," Neil told me.

I nodded.

"They were hooking up a tow strap when we drove past on his throne-mobile," I said, a realization of one complicating factor rising. "The airport has to be five miles from where we are."

"Just about," Neil confirmed.

"We'll never make it there before they lock things down tight," I said.

"Once they find us gone it's going to be hunting season," my friend said.

"We can't fly out of here," I said, disappointed.

It would have been the quickest manner of escape from Perkins and his people. We could be back in Bandon in a few hours. But it wasn't going to happen that way. There would be no sneaking onto the airport grounds to set off in the plane that Dave Arndt had piloted before his death.

Before his murder.

"Perkins doesn't know that," Neil said.

"What?" I pressed, not following where he was going with his statement.

"Perkins will think just what you were," Neil explained. "The plane would be our fastest way out. He'll have people swarming to the south near the airport. And west where you first landed. His people have occupied the northern section of town, so that will be covered."

Now I understood. But I did not like the reality of what my friend was suggesting. Not at all.

"We have to go east," I said.

"Yes," Neil confirmed.

East was away from Bandon. Away from home.

"We'll have to hurry north before the show ends, then cut across the residential areas," Neil said.

I stared at him for a few seconds. Time was precious, I knew. We had to beat the horde of followers who would do Perkins' bidding and hunt us down.

"Detour is the best option," Neil told me.

"I know," I said, looking outside to the dark, deserted streets that would not be that in a very short time. "Let's move."

* * *

It took us three minutes to cross the four-lane avenue just north of our position, and five more to make our way through the brown and dusty yards behind homes in the residential enclave before we turned east, hugging the sides of buildings to shield us from the view of any sentries perched on higher vantage points.

"This one we've gotta cross fast," Neil said as we left a neighborhood and skirted a pair of stores which faced a large boulevard.

"I can't hear the crowd anymore," I said.

"We're too far," Neil reminded me. "We'll know when—
"

And then we knew. To our right as we emerged from between the two stores, the section of the city we'd fled began to light up right before the clanging alarm was sounded. This time it was not to warn of any intruder.

This alert was for us.

"Go," Neil said.

With one arm under his left shoulder we jogged out into the wide street, crossing it at our best speed. Our best, though, wasn't good enough.

"Down!' I shouted, pulling my friend into the gutter on the far side of the boulevard just as the muzzle flashes I'd glimpsed to the south manifested themselves near us as dozens of rounds from automatic rifles tearing into the blacktop.

We were three hundred yards from the intersection where the bank we'd been held in was located. At that distance, in this light, the only explanation was that the sentry located atop that building was equipped with some sort of night vision optics. Whether he'd spotted us and alerted others, or whether others had alerted him to our escape, it was impossible to know.

What was certain, however, was that we had to leave the scant cover I'd dragged us into. And fast. The next volley of shots, without a doubt, would not be wildly sent our way. They would be on target.

"Fletch, we've gotta—"

"I know," I said.

I pulled Neil up, the both of us leaving the gutter and the street behind, running in tandem toward a gutted grocery store just across the sidewalk. We made it inside as the next bursts of automatic fire ricocheted off the building's crumbling brick façade, bits of weathered red stone bursting outward like shrapnel. A sharp sliver of the brick struck me just below my right eye, tearing a short, deep hole in the fleshy part of my cheek.

"Damn!"

I dragged a sleeve across the wound as I swore, then got moving again, helping Neil toward the back of the building. The shotgun was now in my hand, two rounds in it. I had another twelve in my pocket. It was nowhere near enough firepower to win any standoff with the mob Perkins would have descend upon us, so fighting had to be the last of our last resorts.

"Neil, can you run?" I asked. "On your own?"

He drew a breath and nodded, pulling free of my assisting grip as we reached one of three back exits, its door wrenched free of the jamb and lying inside. Beyond I could just make out a parking lot with charred hulks of six cars lined up like victims of some automotive firing squad. I reached into my boot and retrieved the knife, handing it to Neil.

"In case," I said.

"In case," he affirmed, then he ran through the door and into the open swath of blacktop behind the store.

I followed, and once outside the sound of engines racing began to rise. The posse had been set loose on our trail. Which meant we couldn't leave one.

"Hang a left," I said as we crossed from the lot to a cluster of vacant lots surrounded by houses.

"That's north, Fletch," Neil warned me.

"I know."

"His people lay their heads there," Neil said.

"Right," I said. "But they'll all be out looking for us."

Neil thought quickly, reconsidering the plan he'd conceived just moments ago. We'd be making our way into the lion's den, but the lion would be out feeding.

"Hide in plain sight," I said.

"Okay," my friend agreed.

We altered course as the rumble of engines spun up close behind, a trio of vehicles speeding across the parking lot behind the store and continuing on through the vacant lots, splitting up to race down the driveways of the nearby homes. No one appeared to notice us running due north through the rear yards of the neighborhood backing up to the commercial area, and we didn't allow ourselves to stop to look for any pursuers. It was an all out dash, not to freedom, but to safety—temporary as it might be.

"I'm fading, Fletch," Neil said after nearly ten minutes of sprinting and jogging and climbing over fences that had managed to not collapse in the years following the blight.

"One more block," I said.

Next to me I saw his head nod, though his chin was nearly planted upon his chest. He'd left fatigue in the dust a quarter mile behind, and exhaustion just after that. What my friend was pushing against was more than just some physical wall—it was against himself. His body and his mind was screaming at him to stop.

Finally, as we crossed a narrow residential street running east to west, those screams won out and he collapsed on the opposite side of a stone wall after climbing it just behind me.

"Done," Neil said. "Done. Can't...can't..."

He was gasping, but the rush of air was almost a whisper. What strength he'd had was spent, and what I saw now on my friend's face, and in his eyes, was frighteningly familiar. I'd seen it before on our journey back from Cheyenne when sickness and starvation had put him on the verge of death. Here, to come back from this similar state, he would not have to do what he had then, but he could also not go on.

I looked around, appraising our position. We were maybe a mile north of where we'd been held captive, in the backyard of a house with broken windows and missing doors. Large patches of its roof were only partially covered, groups of shingles ripped away, likely by some vicious wind event, leaving stained and sagging plywood sheathing exposed. The place had been open to the elements for years, and did not show any sign of attempted repairs. This was not one of the homes that Perkins' followers would have occupied.

Which meant, for us, it was the best place in a bad situation.

"Let's get you inside," I said.

I helped Neil up, supporting almost his full, thinned-out weight, his feet barely moving as I walked him into the once-pretty home. The back doorway we entered through led into a kitchen, and beyond that a dining room and small living room. It had been a modest house for its onetime occupants, but now was an abandoned, dank shell of its former self.

Neil managed to lift his head. He scanned the space as I did.

"Too exposed," he said.

He wasn't wrong. The front door and windows were missing. Anyone walking by with searching or surveillance in mind could simply shine a light in and see most of the interior.

"There," he said.

I tracked his gaze, which had fixed on a door just off the kitchen.

"Basement," I said, and he nodded.

Eight

The cramped space beneath the small house was damp and dark and cold, all conditions which were difficult, but also necessary at the moment.

"Eat," I told Neil.

I'd positioned my friend on a stack of lumber leftover from some remodeling project. That kept him off the soggy ground. Remnants of discarded drapes still dry in a plastic storage tub provided a makeshift blanket to provide some warmth as he ate the MRE contents shoved in the cargo pocket of his pants. After a few minutes he'd consumed the meager meal, but he'd also begun to show signs of recovery.

"Dry and stale," Neil said. "Meals Rarely Edible lives up to its name."

Dry...

He needed water. We both did. But there was no source to provide any. No running taps in the kitchen, and any that had gathered in puddles within the house would be fouled beyond any filtering we could manage.

"How far do you think the river is?" I asked him.

Neil shook his head then let it rest against the stone foundation wall behind him.

"Too far," he said. "I'm okay. We'll come across a stream to the east."

"Sure," I said, unconvinced by that likelihood. "But when? You're in no shape to move right now."

"I can argue against your position," he feigned challenging me.

"You'd lose," I said.

"Yeah," he admitted. "I would."

I lowered myself onto the lumber pile and sat with my friend in silence. There was no sound at all. No hint of the pursuit we'd evaded.

But there would be. This I knew.

"He's going to come hard at us, Fletch."

"I know," I said.

We were the key to his plans. Or what he believed we knew was. What, though, did we actually know? What did *my friend* know?

"Where is it, Neil?"

He looked to me, saying nothing for a moment.

"Are you sure that's a question you want the answer to?" he asked.

"I do," I said.

Neil shifted his position, sitting straighter. Eyeing me unlike he ever had, it was not my friend looking at me right then—it was the possessor of a secret. The keeper of some terrible knowledge.

"Ty Olin got the sample of Four Eleven," Neil said, referencing the identifier of the original biologic agent which caused the blight.

"And you got Four Twelve," I said, stating the conventional wisdom amongst those who had any knowledge of the covert operations to secure the pair of deadly pathogens.

"I was supposed to," Neil said.

Now I straightened where I sat, absorbing what my friend had just hinted at—that Four Twelve didn't exist.

"Four Twelve was a lie?" I pressed him.

He thought for a moment, taking time to choose his words, something he'd rarely, if ever, done with me. We were close enough to speak freely, and always had been.

Not for this, it appeared.

"I was with a SEAL Team that raided a lab—"

"Olin shared that," I interrupted my friend. "Was he lying, or did he just believe a lie?"

"Did he tell you what things were like in D.C. as the blight spread?"

"Factions forming," I said, recalling Olin's words from our first meeting. "Power grabs. Everything was going to hell. So the government released the blight sample he secured on its own to force a faster collapse of civilization."

Neil nodded, and it seemed to me there was some shame in the gesture. Some apology, even.

"We weren't living up to what we were supposed to do," he said. "Or be."

"What the hell happened, Neil? With you? With this sample of Four Twelve you supposedly ran off with?"

My friend shook his head, his thoughts seeming to drift back to that time. To when his lie began.

"We raided the lab," Neil explained. "There was no one there. It had been abandoned. There was just leftover equipment and compounds."

"I don't understand," I said. "If it was abandoned..."

"I didn't want it to be abandoned, Fletch. I was planning on Four Twelve being there. I was counting on getting that sample so I could leverage it."

I processed what he was saying, which paralleled suspicions that he'd planned to give Four Twelve to the nascent Unified Government forces to counter its use by our own leadership.

"Mutually Assured Destruction," I suggested.

"Essentially," he confirmed. "Only no one would have the button to push."

In that snippet of his explanation I understood both the truth of the matter and the misconceptions which had developed around his actions. My friend was not going to hand the deadly virus to either side.

"You were going to keep it for yourself," I said. "As a doomsday threat."

"Hell of a plan to hatch in the middle of an apocalypse, right?"

It was a thin attempt at self-deprecation. Neither of us reacted with anything close to a laugh.

"I figured if both sides thought the other might have it…"

"They each might dial down any likelihood of outright conflict," I said, completing the suggestion for him.

"It was a chance," he said. "But when there was nothing there to give that the threat I could wield any credence, I created it. I told the SEALs with me that I found the sample."

"Red water with organic compounds?" I asked, once more drawing on what Olin had told me.

Neil smiled at me.

"Organic compounds," he repeated. "The red water thing you got from that message I slipped you, but the rest had to come from Ty Olin."

The hidden instructions on how to craft a facsimile to Four Twelve had reached me inside Krista's book of drawings. I'd used that to threaten General Weatherly and end the siege of Bandon. I'd had no idea then that it was only a lie based upon another lie.

"Olin also said you killed your superior when she came looking for the real sample," I said.

According to Neil's former CIA colleague, after the agency lab had discovered that the vial of Four Twelve they'd been given was nothing remotely dangerous, his handler had been dispatched to the Virginia farm where he resided with his ailing elderly father. What happened there, Olin had said, was the outright elimination of a woman ready to expose his actions. All that was hearsay to this point. I wanted confirmation, or denial.

What I received was a mixture of both.

"I didn't kill Allison Millbank," Neil said, confirming the name Olin had shared with me. "My father did."

"What?"

My friend had told me after reaching my refuge in Montana that his father, not wanting to suffer through the cancer that was killing him, had taken his own life so that his son would be free of any burden to care for him as the blight ravaged the world. I'd believed him then. But then I'd believed much of what he'd told me. Too much, it appeared.

"She drew a weapon when I wouldn't give her the answer she wanted about Four Twelve," Neil said. "My father heard the argument, came up behind her, and put two rounds in her head."

I let that sink in. Dieter Moore would do anything to protect his son. Anything. And it seemed he had.

And continued to do so with his next action.

"He told me I had to leave," Neil said. "I'd never outright told him what I did, but he sensed that there was more to my work than what was on the surface. He knew people would be coming when Allison didn't return to Langley. He also knew I wouldn't leave him there to die."

"So he did kill himself," I said, hoping that was not just another piece of the larger lie.

Neil nodded, and I saw truth in the silent gesture. He coughed, a dry hacking that he tried to silence by burying his mouth against his arm.

"You all right?" I asked.

"All the talking is drying me out," he said.

There were clouds building to the west when we'd reached the house. A spring storm was a possibility. With a suitably clean container we could capture some rain to drink. I scanned the basement, but saw nothing that could be used, the toppled shelving having spilled only old paint cans on the floor.

"I'm going to see if I can find something to catch rain," I told him as I stood, shotgun in hand.

"Rain is fifty-fifty at best," he said.

"You a weatherman now?"

"Fifty bucks says not a drop falls," he challenged me.

"You're on," I said, looking to the stairs. "I'm going to check upstairs. If there's nothing there I'll scrounge at the neighbors for something to set out in the back yard."

"Be careful," Neil told me. "They're going to be looking for us."

"They've got a lot of ground to cover," I said. "We put some space between us and them."

Neil considered my assurance for a moment, then nodded.

"Still be careful," he said. "We're not soldiers, but we're damn sure behind enemy lines."

"I know," I said, then I made my way upstairs, leaving my friend behind.

Nine

The abandoned house we had taken refuge in was that way for a reason, I learned. Everything of use had been stripped or stolen. Not a single cupboard in the kitchen held anything that could be used to catch rain for drinking water. Nothing in the single bathroom was any more useful. No dusty but useable vases or bowls were to be found in the living room.

I was going to have to venture outside to another house.

At the front door I stood, looking to the street and the neighborhood beyond. No house on this block, or the ones I could see to the south and the north, had been occupied by Perkins' people. We were likely a half mile past the inhabited zone, I estimated. Eventually, though, some search would be made of this area, though how involved it would be was debatable. Perkins might want every square inch of Klamath Falls searched, from the basements to the rafters, but reality stood in the way of that. He had only so many people, and, if I put myself in his shoes, I would concentrate my efforts on our last known direction of travel. We'd been moving east when we lost our pursuers, and that was where I expected the bulk of his people to be focused.

I stepped from the house, onto the rickety porch, boards beneath me creaking and cracking. The columns that supported its roof and old lattice added for privacy from the sides afforded me some cover where I stood, but I knew I needed to make a decision and move. My choices were fairly straightforward—go left, go right, or go straight. The latter was the least desirable since it would mean crossing the dusty yard, and then the street to reach the houses on the opposite side.

But it also held the most promise, I thought. A pair of structures directly across from where I stood looked to be in better condition than any of the surrounding houses. Why that was I didn't know. Perhaps their owners had lasted longer than others in the neighborhood and were able to fend off scavengers and intruders. Whatever the reason, despite the risk, I decided that the most fruitful course of action was to start my search there.

I stepped to the edge of the porch and peered fully past the lattice. In the distance I could see lights, but they were stationary, and had to come from the search expanding to the south of us. There was no indication of any threat nearby. If there was going to be a time of minimum risk, it was now.

With steady quickness I left the porch and moved quickly across the yard, then the street, not sprinting. There was no point in risking a trip and fall in the dark on some uneven piece of concrete or buckled asphalt. In less than twenty seconds I was at the front door of the first house.

Or where the door had been. Despite its appearance from across the street, the building had been violated, though not to the extent of those nearby. The front door had long ago been kicked in, splinters of the jamb and its broken strike plate on the floor. I stepped in and saw more familiar sights—upturned furniture, broken windows, and evidence of weather infiltrating through untended leaks in the roof.

I held the shotgun at the ready out of habit as I moved deeper into the house, leaving the front room and finding the kitchen. The cabinets here were all open and stripped bare. Bits of broken glass and plates crunched beneath my boots. The hope that I'd had when surveying the place from a distance began to fade. From within the home looked little different from the one I'd left Neil in.

Garage...

I saw the shape of the structure behind the house through the back doorway, no door left there, the hinges stripped away. Beyond that an alley ran behind the houses, providing access to the single-car garages. I stepped out and into the back yard and began moving toward the small structure ahead. But I never made it.

Light suddenly filled the narrow avenue behind the garage, coming from my right, its source in motion.

A vehicle...

My confidence that we were beyond the area of concern had been misguided, if not outright foolish. Perkins was not going to simply fall for our deceptive move to the east. He was, as we feared, sending his people in every direction to hunt us down.

I turned quickly and ran back into the house, taking cover just inside the back door and peering cautiously out at an angle, catching sight of an old passenger van, spotlights blazing from its missing side windows. It was illuminating the back yards of houses as it cruised slowly northward. No doubt there were armed people behind the glare of the lights, ready to fire upon anything they saw. Upon anyone they saw.

Once the vehicle was past I slipped away from the door and hurried toward the front of the house, but there I was again stopped by what lay ahead. More lights, in the street out front. They were headlights of a dark pickup stopped in the middle of the street, one house south of my location.

And there were men. Armed men. Three of them that I could see. One stood at the open driver's door of the idling truck, on watch, rifle in hand. The other two had split from their transport, one heading to a house on the west side of the street, and the other to a house on the east.

The house directly south of where I stood.

Damn...

It was a two-pronged search they were running. Lights on one side to, hopefully, spot or flush out the captives who'd escaped, and more overt searchers on the opposite side to survey the interiors of every building. Perkins had committed a large number of his people to the effort, and would press them until they had results.

Until they had us.

I had to get back to Neil. He was in no shape to handle an armed adversary. But between him and me were at least three men with the weaponry to end either of us should we resist. They wanted us back in their leader's hands. Back in captivity. Back to those cages where we would be tormented and tortured.

That wasn't going to happen.

I sidestepped into the hallway just off the living room and waited, watching from the shadows as the man across the street emerged from the house he'd just searched and gave a wave to his comrade standing watch at the truck. At the same instant I heard footsteps. Heavy boots mounting the steps and crossing the porch. I eased back fully into the darkness filling the hallway and raised the shotgun, twin barrels over my right shoulder, stock facing forward as I slowed my breathing. Seeking a sense of calm as the moment of confrontation neared.

The footsteps were inside now. They paused, the man who'd come to search the house taking a moment to scan the interior from where he stood. Should he move no deeper into the house and simply brand it empty, leaving to continue on to the neighboring property, the plan I'd hastily crafted would be upset.

But he did not. The footsteps began again, drawing nearer. He was not heading for the kitchen and the back door. He was making his way toward the bedrooms.

Toward me.

My grip tightened on the shotgun as I drew it further back, building a powerful strike, one which I unleashed as the man came around the entry into the hall. For an instant we were face to face in the dark corridor, close enough that a wash of recognition and surprise showed just before the butt of the shotgun stock smashed hard against his face, cratering his skull. He fell backwards at an angle, sliding down the hallway's wall until he sat awkwardly, head tipped to one side, the AK 47 he'd wielded settled gently across his lap.

I struck him a second time, and a third, the splatter of his blood spraying wet across my face. He toppled fully to the floor now and I seized his AK, taking the two additional magazines he had in a belt pouch and leaving the shotgun next to him. I had firepower now, real firepower, but to use it would be to alert everyone within a half mile, and I couldn't do that. This had to go down as I envisioned, or we'd be done.

I slipped past the man's body and back into the living room, maintaining cover as I peered through a window to the street outside and the houses beyond. The other searcher came out and, once again, waved to the pickup's driver, then made his way to the house where my friend was waiting in the basement. As soon as he was inside I made my move.

The driver who'd been standing watch in the middle of the street was on the opposite side of the pickup and his attention was focused almost entirely on that side. As I came out of the house and crossed the front yard, I was prepared to fire at him should he turn my way. I was prepared to fire at anyone who might see me. But there was no one else, just the driver, holding his position, oblivious as I came around the back of the truck and, as I had before, turned the weapon I wielded around and used the solid wood butt of the stock to deliver a deadly blow to the back of his head.

He dropped like a forgotten doll, his own AK clanking to the pavement as blood spread quickly beneath him. I had hoped this elimination would be as quiet as the first, but it wasn't, and I ran quickly toward the house where Neil was before the searcher within might react to the sound from outside.

I didn't get there in time.

"Freeze," the man said as he stepped from the doorway, his AK 47 shouldered and aimed at my chest. "Drop it."

He wasn't yelling. Wasn't reacting with fury to what he must see past where I'd stopped just shy of the porch. His comrade's body lay dead in the street, and he clearly had to assume that the third member of their patrol had met a similar fate. Still, he did not explode at me. He had a mission, an objective, and he understood what that meant. Recapturing us was the imperative.

"I said drop it," he repeated.

I'd already stopped my advance, and now I had to surrender my weapon. And once I did it would be over. If I were to resist, I would be shot before I could bring the AK I'd taken to bear.

You can't go back...

That thought flashed in my head. Going back would mean eventual death. Here, though, death would come quickly. I had a decision to make.

But, as it turned out, another option presented itself out of the blue.

The man tensed suddenly and his head jerked backward, the AK rising, its aim coming off me just as it loosed a long burst of automatic fire that stitched into the air and shredded the porch roof as he fell backward, finger coming off the trigger as his body dropped and came to rest at Neil's feet, a bloody knife in my friend's hand.

"We've gotta move," he said.

He'd saved my life, and his own, by somehow summoning enough strength to do what had to be done. As he crouched and took the dead man's AK he looked to me where I stood, still.

"Fletch..."

I couldn't imagine how he'd done what he just had, plunging a knife into the soft spot at the base of the man's skull to scramble his cerebellum. It had to be the same thing within that had allowed him to let his body wither so he might escape. My friend, who I'd always known was a different kind of person, was more than that. He was singular.

"Let's go," he said, weapon in hand as he came to me.

I nodded and we hurried to the truck as the sound of engines racing seemed to build in every direction.

Ten

Neil slipped in behind the wheel and I took the seat next to him.

"The whole world's coming down on us, buddy," he said as he floored the pickup and swung the wheel left, steering us down the driveway of the house next to the one we'd taken refuge in. "It's going to get bumpy."

The truck fishtailed down the narrow driveway, rear of the bed bouncing off a pair of old fenceposts, the once stout supports shattering after years of weathering. Ahead of us an old, leaning fence made of dogeared redwood boards separated the property from the alley behind it. Neil never slowed, punching through the weakened barrier and then through a similar fence on the opposite side, driving us down the side of yet another house until we reached the street in front of it.

"Reload me," he said as he turned, heading south on the residential street.

I took the AK that he'd acquired, half its magazine spent by the man he'd killed, ejecting that and inserting one that I'd taken from the man who'd died at my hand.

"I'll see what we've got," I said as he sped south, then turned west on a connecting street.

The inventory took just a minute. We had five spare magazines for the AKs, a pair of flashlights, two canteens in a shoulder bag, and two cans of beans, one open in the truck's cupholder on the passenger side.

"Add this to the collection," Neil said, tossing the bloody knife onto the bag where I had gathered the meager supplies.

"What's the plan?" I asked.

"The plan is west," he answered. "Only issue is I don't know where the hell the best way west is."

Ahead, through the dim night, a large intersection came into view. An intersection I recognized.

"Take a right up there at that old gas station," I said.

"You have a map?"

I shook my head at my friend's ribbing challenge.

"Perkins brought me in past that," I told him. "I had a great view from the back of his throne-mobile. We came across a bridge. It's north of here. It crosses the river and the road heads west into the hills."

"Outstanding," he said.

He turned us right, the faint outline of the span across the Klamath river ahead and to our left as we drove north, no adversaries in sight.

"They're in confusion," Neil said as he accelerated. "And that's a beautiful thing."

I suspected that was the spy in my friend talking. The persona that might have worked to foment discord in a foreign land. Whether that skillset was worth anything in this situation was yet to be determined. And hopefully it wouldn't matter one way or the other as we made our way to Bandon.

"What's the fuel situation?" I asked.

"Half a tank," Neil answered after a glance at the unlit dash of the blacked-out pickup.

"That's not enough to reach Bandon," I observed.

"If there's even a viable road to get us there," Neil commented. "Let's just worry about—"

The muzzle flashes ahead cut off all discussion, a base of fire directed at us from the east end of the bridge. Neil swung hard left into a parking lot, a few rounds ripping into the truck bed five feet behind us.

"There goes the bridge idea," he said.

He floored it and crossed the lot, bouncing over the curb and back onto the road, speeding back the way we'd come, more wild fire flashing behind us.

"Just keep going straight," I said.

My friend passed the turn where we'd entered the wide road at the gas station, paralleling the Klamath River as I turned and bashed the rear window of the cab out with the butt of my AK. I slipped the barrel through and planted my knees on the bench seat, facing backward as two pairs of headlights blazed to life near the bridge. I held my fire, not wanting to announce our position unless it was absolutely necessary.

"They're on the move," I said.

"Moving is better than moving and shooting," Neil said.

That fact remained in effect for just a second more as muzzle flashes pulsed again from the vehicle now pursuing us two hundred yards back, near misses whizzing past or clicking off the asphalt as the long shots reached us. They would be trucks of some sort, I knew, with the passengers in back firing over the cab as the driver focused on running us down.

"Fletch, ahead," Neil said.

I looked over my shoulder and saw what had caught my friend's attention. Two blocks from our position a wash of light was building from an intersecting street to the east. The meaning of what we saw was as plain to me as it was to him—more vehicles were moving to cut us off.

"Hold tight," he said.

Without further explanation he turned hard left at the nearest intersection, steering us away from both the pursuers behind and the intercepting vehicles ahead. As we quickly discovered, though, every route of evasion was an avenue to conflict.

"North side ahead!"

Neil warned me of the threat on his side of the pickup. I looked quickly and fixed on the van at the side of the road, a trio of figures outside. He floored the accelerator and I angled my AK's aim toward the enemy vehicle as we passed, shots erupting from the surprised shooters. I squeezed the trigger and held it down, adjusting my long burst back and forth, raking their position. A pair of incoming rounds punched through the roof of the pickup after sailing right past my face, but my suppressing fire sent the three who'd opened up on us scattering for cover.

"Get us clear of this," I said, easing off the trigger with maybe a third of my magazine remaining.

"Trying, buddy," Neil said.

He turned us again, south this time, then immediately east again, bouncing through dips in an intersection before, once more, taking a southerly direction. The throaty roar of the diesel powerplant beneath the hood was deafening at full speed, but not so much that the distinctive crack didn't reach us, sounding sharp from the west.

"Long rifle," I said.

Neil began to swerve the pickup back and forth, jerking from curb to curb along the residential street in anticipation of what came next, rounds impacting as the would-be sniper dialed in their aim.

"It's from the bank," Neil said.

I shifted to look that way, now northwest from our moving position, and could see both the silhouette of the building's high top, and muzzle flashes spaced about every three seconds. We'd suspected that someone atop that structure had spotted us with some sort of optics made to cut through the darkness, and now it was clear that such a device was mounted atop a precision rifle.

"They can't shoot worth a damn," Neil said.

It was true what he said. The marksman was not that, sending rounds at us that were only 'close', not 'on target'.

"He only needs a lucky shot," I reminded my friend.

"No, all he needs is to radio everyone and tell them where we are," Neil said.

It had to be assumed that Perkins' people would have some communication ability among those they'd sent after us. No one was bothering with bells or radio clicks to send warnings about us. They'd be broadcasting in the open, sharing our location immediately as it became available.

PLINK!

The lucky shot finally found us. Some good fortune was still on our side, though, the round punching a single hole in the left front of the hood, seeming to miss anything vital in the engine compartment.

"Damn!"

Neil swore as he jerked the pickup to the right to avoid a pile of old tires seemingly meant as a barricade long ago. Without using the vehicle's headlights, obstacles could become collisions with little warning. This one he missed by inches, straightening out again past the makeshift barrier before resuming his side to side swerving.

"He's not shooting anymore," Neil said after a moment.

I looked again in the direction of the bank building and saw that the terrain of this neighborhood had sloped downhill, obscuring us from view.

"We're blocked," I told him.

"Good," he commented, turning now, taking a side street to the east. "We've gotta use the cover while we have it."

I maintained my watch out the rear of the cab, wisps of light flashing briefly over the houses on the south side of the street.

"They're back there," I reported. "Out of sight."

"Are they on our trail?"

I considered his question as I watched the beams from the headlights drift in and out of view.

"No," I said, making some mental approximations based upon the motion of the light's sources. "They're running patterns, it looks like. Up one block, then cut over to another."

I heard my friend let out a breath as he turned south once more, our position still low enough that we could not be seen by the gunman atop the bank building.

"There may still be lookouts this way," he said. "If there are, they won't engage us. They'll just call in everything on wheels."

"That's out of our hands," I said.

Neil turned to me as he drove and in that instant I saw something familiar in his eyes. It was the same cold surety I'd been witness to when he'd executed the cannibals discovered in a shack near my old refuge in Montana.

"If you see a lookout, Fletch, kill them. Even if they don't have a weapon. Just kill them."

He looked back to the road ahead and kept us heading south. What he'd said didn't shock me, but it did sober my sense of our reunion. This wasn't two old friends getting together at some picnic in the park after a long separation. It was a fight for survival. Any illusions beyond that I had to put away for a later time.

"We're gonna make it," I told my friend.

Then I turned and scanned the way we'd come, houses thinning out as we began to leave Klamath Falls and our pursuers behind.

For now.

Eleven

An old sign with barely any paint visible marked the two lanes we were speeding along as Highway 39. Another informed us that the California border was less than five miles distant.

"Anything, Fletch?"

I looked behind once again. There wasn't even a hint of headlights or any presence whatsoever in the night.

"Nothing," I reported.

I felt the pickup slow, Neil easing off the accelerator, our speed dropping by half. We couldn't fully relax, but for the moment we could catch our breath. And more.

"Here," I said, taking the open can of beans from the cupholder. "Down this."

Neil eyed the offering for a moment.

"What if the guy had syphilis?"

I allowed a half chuckle at his quip.

"Then enjoy your beans and syphilis," I said.

My friend took the can and tipped the contents into his mouth as he drove, emptying it in three swallows. I opened the second can from the shoulder bag, discarding the pop top on the floor before handing it over.

"I'm gonna be fun in closed quarters tonight, Fletch."

"Like I wouldn't already know that, gas master," I said.

We'd spent too many hours together as disgusting teenagers to not know which one of us could unleash a pungent hell after ingesting the proper amount of beans or chili. Neil was the clear top of the heap in that category. I smiled at those memories. Then, I was just smiling, simply because he was here. With me.

But as fulfilling as that moment was for me, I knew what lay ahead for my friend when we returned to Bandon. It would be, in many ways, painful. More so than joyous. Grace, too, would be shattered by this impossible revelation. Neil Moore had come back from the dead, and with that reappearance came all the emotional baggage one could imagine. And some none of us could.

"Fletch..."

"Yeah?"

"Are you sure that plane that spooked our hosts wasn't from Bandon?"

"Positive," I answered.

He considered that for a moment, his head shaking slightly.

"If that wasn't someone out looking for you, then it was someone else out looking," he said. "And there's a lot of nowhere out there that someone can fly a plane around and look, but this someone zeroed in on Klamath Falls. At night."

All that he said was true, and, in its own way, troubling. The unknown had, more often than not, led to events which were unpleasant at best, and deadly at worst.

"Someone was scouting with a purpose, Fletch."

"I know," I said. "But is that really something for us to worry about right now?"

He quieted and shook his head, slowing the pickup to a crawl. I looked to see what had brought us to a near stop.

"Bridge," he said.

"I'll get out," I said.

He stopped and put the truck in park. I climbed out and, with my AK in one hand, walked forward toward the narrow span, just two lanes crossing a minor canal or stream. Except it did not.

Even in the weak moonlight it was plain what lay ahead. Just yards from dry land the structure had crumbled, huge chunks of concrete fallen into the flowing waters, creating a mini dam which the current rushed over. I looked back to my friend and shook my head.

"The road slips off to the left over here," Neil said when I returned to the pickup, pointing out his window.

I looked and saw the shadowed silhouettes of low buildings to the northeast.

"We can avoid the town if we stay close to the stream," I suggested.

Steering clear of any contact at this point was preferable, even if it happened to be some stray group of survivors, however unlikely that might be. Eyes that could see us would be attached to mouths that could share what had been seen should Perkins come calling.

"Sounds good," Neil said.

He backed up a bit and then turned east onto the gravel road that paralleled the stream. Rocks clicked off the fenders as we cruised through the darkness. I kept a watchful eye to the north, looking past my friend as he drove, the backs of buildings a few dozen yards distant. The night made the town appear as just a collection of boxy shadows. In the daylight it would be worse, I knew. The sun would reveal the harsh realities of a dead place. A place waiting to be weathered away, eroded by rain and wind like mountains had been for eons. This place, whatever its name was, would not last that long.

"Can Bandon hold him off?" Neil asked.

The question came out of nowhere, but it was not hard for me to understand the true 'why' of it. He was worried about the family he'd left behind. The family I was certain he now believed he'd lost.

"We're strong," I assured him. "He doesn't have any secret weapon to use."

Neil nodded and steered around a deep rut in the road.

"Good," he said.

I waited, saying nothing, giving him the chance to speak more on the matter. But he didn't. I suspected he couldn't. Not right then. The news I'd shared with him about Grace hadn't just opened some old would—it hade created a new one. A cut that was deep and raw.

"It's going to work out," I said as the silence lingered. "It will."

He didn't respond to my words. Instead he stayed focused on the dark road ahead, his gaze slack, more from dammed emotion than fatigue right then.

"Neil..."

"Fletch, later, okay?"

The relationship we'd always shared, one of direct truthfulness, had to be put on hold. For a while, at least. As hard as that was, I had to respect what he wanted. What he *needed*.

"I'd trade a steak dinner for a map about—"

BTHUNK!

The sound was deafening, and the impact that caused it jolted the pickup, literally lifting the right front in the air after a brief dip into the hole neither of us had noticed in the dark. A sickening shriek rose from the engine compartment as the steering wheel whipped back and forth in Neil's grip.

"Something broke," he said. "Big time."

He didn't even steer the vehicle to the side of the gravel road. It simply rolled that way, the only control he maintained was the brake, which was pressed to the floorboard until our forward motion stopped fully.

"We can see if there's a garage open at this hour," I said, injecting some gallows humor to the plainly humorless moment.

"Our luck they'd only take cash," Neil quipped right back at me.

We stepped from the pickup and surveyed the damage. The nose of the pickup had settled low on the right side, the corresponding front wheel twisted severely to the left, away from the direction we'd rolled.

"Tie rod had to snap," I said.

"Spring and shock didn't fare much better," Neil added.

There was something else, though. Something we smelled first, the acrid scent of burnt diesel hitting us just before the pop and the flash of fire erupted.

Twelve

The unseen rut in the road had done more than disable our suspension and steering. Something under the old diesel's hood had broken and caused a fire, oil or fuel flashing on the hot engine to send smoke billowing and flames licking from the front wheel wells.

"Get the gear," I said.

Neil and I both returned to the vehicle, reaching in through the front doors we'd left open to retrieve the two AKs we'd wielded, along with the shoulder bag, canteens, and five spare magazines. It wasn't remotely enough to sustain us, but it would have to do until we could manage that for ourselves.

"This thing's going to mark our position for five miles," Neil said, the glow of the now raging fire building. "Twenty when the sun comes up and that smoke column becomes visible."

I nodded and thought, the sound of flowing water bringing an idea to the surface. A possibility.

"We push it into the stream," I suggested.

Neil thought for a moment, looking toward the tributary which had altered our course of travel. Below the bank it was impossible to see if we could maneuver the truck that far, the light from the fire blocked by the bulging embankment. My friend reached into the truck quickly, recoiling from the building inferno, and returning to where I stood nearer the stream with a flashlight in his hand. At another time neither of us would have chanced using the light, lest its beam aid in marking our position. But with the vehicular bonfire beginning to rage twenty feet from us it could do little to make things worse.

He activated the light and directed it down toward the water, what it revealed immediately ending any thoughts of forcing the truck to freewheel down into the stream with us pushing. The remnants of thick stumps rose high on the embankment like bollards used to block vehicles from entering restricted areas.

"It's just gonna burn, Fletch."

He turned the flashlight off, but before he did the beam shifted, illuminating the opposite shore for an instant.

"Wait," I said, snatching the light from him and turning it on again. "Look."

He tracked the beam and saw what I had, resting inverted atop the opposite bank.

"A boat," Neil said.

It was dull and metal, like the one we'd used long ago to cross the Green River with Elaine as we sought the cure for the blight near Cheyenne. Some amount of dust had accumulated along one side of the upturned craft, a dirty drift crafted by years of wind and weather. But from fifty feet away it still looked viable. The only way to know for sure, though, was from up close.

"We have to cross this stream," I said.

Neil thought for a moment.

"This has to flow south," he said. "It's southwest right now, but it has to make a turn toward California."

I'd spent enough time scouting the terrain in the south of Oregon to suspect he was right. This far inland, the waterways would not be flowing toward the Columbia River or the Pacific. They would be meandering through farmlands toward the border.

"I know south isn't the best direction," my friend said.

"Actually, it's not terrible," I said. "If we can get south to California and then turn west to the coast, we can make it north to Bandon. No map necessary."

"Boat then walk?" Neil suggested.

I nodded.

"If it floats," I said

"Let's find out," he said.

I slung the bag over my shoulder, the weight of the canteens and extra mags more nuisance than burden. We each held our own rifles as we sidestepped down the embankment, its slope turning from dry and dusty to sloppy mud where the water sloshed upon it.

"The current doesn't look bad," Neil said.

"Runoff hasn't peaked yet," I said.

Without knowing the snowpack from the previous winter, it was impossible to tell when the bulk of the spring melt would make its way to where we stood. But there was a steady current, I could see. Steady but manageable.

"You're okay doing this?" I asked my friend.

"Eighty percent," he assured me.

I imagined he was referring to his strength. The food he'd eaten since our escape, both from Jake's MRE and the open can of beans left in the truck, had given him a burst of energy. But that was temporary. Still, there was little choice but to press on as quickly as we could. I would have to keep an eye on him, though. And, in an oddly comforting way, despite his fragile state, I knew he'd be doing the same for me.

"I'll go first," I said.

My first step into the water soaked me to the knee, and the second submerged me in the chilly water to the waist. But, as Neil had estimated, the current was not unmanageable. I was halfway across the thirty-foot body of flowing water when I looked back and saw my friend stepping into the stream.

"It's only waist deep," I shouted back to him.

He held his AK at chest level, keeping it dry, and worked his way toward where I stood, handling the gentle rush of water with ease.

Until the unseen log floated into him from upstream and he disappeared beneath the surface.

"Neil!"

I unslung the bag and tossed it and my own AK to the soggy bank ahead, then turned back to where my friend had been. The glow of the fire raging above the embankment flickered upon the moving water, and in that weak, stuttering I light I caught a glimpse of movement at least twenty feet downstream from where Neil had last been. It was it arm, and his hand, the AK still in its grip, held above the water. The fool was trying to keep his weapon dry instead of saving himself.

"Neil!"

I shouted his name and dove into the water at a gentle angle, swimming in the shallows toward him. With each breath I took as my head popped above the water I could see Neil struggling, trying to get his footing as the current continued to push him away from me. And still, as he flailed and tumbled, he kept hold of his AK.

"Drop the weapon," I shouted after a quick breath.

He didn't listen. The beefy AK seemed to act like an anchor, pulling him down every time he almost managed to get upright again. His strength, almost nonexistent as we began to cross the stream, had to be at its lowest.

His will to live, and to fight, though, was not.

I'd closed about half the distance to him, just a ten-foot gap remaining when he stopped, his feet finding purchase on a solid patch of the stream bed. I spun my body and jammed my boots into the soft floor of the waterway and grabbed my friend's shirt as we, once again, stood next to each other.

"You're crazy," I said, gulping air and eyeing his AK.

To that he shook his dripping head.

"I'm not ending up unarmed again," he told me, his gaze steely and certain. "Not a chance."

I couldn't argue with his desire but risking his life as he had just felt wrong. That was my problem, I knew, the brief time we'd had together since being miraculously reunited coloring my reaction. To see him almost swept away was horrific, and the bottom line was I couldn't imagine losing my friend. Again.

"Let's get out of this," I said.

I held his shirt with an iron grip as we both trudged toward the edge of the stream. We made it to the bank and clawed our way up the slope, catching our breath at the top of the embankment. Half a football field was a conservative guess as to how far we'd been pushed downstream, and from that vantage point it was made very clear just how precarious our situation was.

"They're not going to miss that," Neil said.

My gaze had fixed on the inferno we'd left behind as well. The pickup no longer resembled anything like a vehicle. It was simply a wide, roiling column of hot orange fire spitting flames into the night sky. Neil had said the smoke from it would be easily seen for twenty miles once the sun came up. I didn't think it would take our pursuers that long to see what we were.

"That boat better be viable," I said.

I stood and helped my friend up, both of us cold and soaked. The night was mild, so hypothermia wasn't an immediate concern. Not for me. Neil's starved body would be more susceptible to those effects, so, at some point, we'd have to deal with that.

Now, though, we had to put some serious miles between us and the burning truck.

It took us only two minutes to reach the boat. I gathered the bag and my weapon from the bank just below it as Neil set his AK down and surveyed the aluminum craft.

"No holes that I can see," he said.

"The seams could be bad," I reminded him, running a hand along the riveted sections where pieces of the old boat had been assembled.

"One way to find out," he said.

"I'll get it," I told him, crouching and gripping the edge before lifting and flipping it onto its keel.

"Jesus..."

Neil's exclamation was quiet, almost reverent. I offered no reaction to what was revealed when the boat was moved.

It was a body. A man, I thought, amazingly intact clothes still shrouding the nearly skeletal frame. He'd died long after the blight had ravaged the world. There was no evidence of animal predation, and no insect infestation. Through the years beneath the boat, as winter and summer repeated, his skin and flesh was dried and frozen repeatedly, leaving a hideously preserved mimic of what he had been in life. It was not unlike the body I'd seen just outside the school gymnasium as Perkins took me to bear witness to the horror he'd concocted, but still I was made uneasy by the sight. And what it meant about this man.

"He was hiding," I said.

Neil nodded. The man had nothing, just two paddles clutched close to his chest.

"From what?" Neil wondered.

"Does it matter?"

My friend shook his head and picked up his AK.

"Let's get it in the water," he said.

I gently slipped the paddles from the man's grip and set them in the boat, the both of us guiding it down the embankment and into the stream. We climbed in, Neil nearest the bow as we began to paddle away from the blazing wreck. I glanced back to take a final look and was instantly horrified.

"The boat left a mark," I said.

Neil stopped paddling and turned, the current the only force propelling us now.

"What do you mean?"

"Around the body," I said. "There's an impression."

It was unmistakably the shape of an upturned boat surrounding the corpse, something no one would have trouble identifying.

"If they find the truck, they'll spot that," I said.

"Forget it, Fletch. If we stop and go back and try to cover it up, it's going to look like something was covered up. They're going to know anyway. Perkins is barely human, but he's not dumb."

Neil began paddling again. He was right about trying to cover our tracks. It would be futile. And, with no idea how far behind us any pursuers might be, even making the attempt could prove not only foolish, but fatal.

"All right," I said.

I began paddling again, joining my friend in propelling the small craft away from the inferno. It was not a perfect situation by a long shot, but we'd rarely had the stars align fully in our favor. And in those instances we'd come through. We'd survived.

Thirteen

The stream meandered, switching back on itself, tracking east, then west again after a sharp bend through flat terrain which had once been thriving farm fields, finally settling on a generally southeasterly course of flow. We let the current do most of the work, paddling only when necessary. By the time the first hints of the new day lay as a blue line on the eastern horizon we'd had to climb from the boat four times and maneuver it over obstacles which had fallen into the waterway, creating mini dams which the stream spilled over.

Not every bridge or pipeline crossing the stream had collapsed, though. One narrow bridge we reached as the sun peeked above the edge of the earth to our left still stood, and, without saying a word, each of us began backpaddling against the current until we were stopped along the shore.

"Welcome to California," I said, reading the faded graffiti which someone had scrawled upon the edge of the concrete span, just enough of the pre-blight marking left to be readable.

"This is just going to keep heading south," Neil said. "Until it dumps into a lake or a bigger river."

The latter was the worse option. All we needed was to be suddenly faced with riding an aluminum boat through whitewater created by unregulated runoff. The land was turning wild again, and with it the rivers which had once raged freely, flooding and menacing those who were foolish enough to test themselves against it.

"Let's just put a few more miles between us and Perkins," I suggested. "Then we can hoof it west."

That would be the beginning of a journey unto itself. One not unlike our return from Cheyenne. We were poorly supplied then, as we were now. But we were also closer to home. And, with any luck, those who now knew that we were missing—that I was missing—would send people looking for us, most likely Beekman in a plane scouring the landscape from above.

That belief presented a particularly vexing problem.

"We've gotta be careful," I said to Neil as we paddled away from the shore and rejoined the current. "Bandon will eventually send someone by air to look, but so will Perkins, I imagine. And then there's the night flyer."

"Making ourselves visible to the wrong one could be a fatal mistake," Neil said. "Or not doing that."

We could just as easily hide from Beekman as mistakenly signal those certainly hunting us down at this very moment. There was one further question, though, and Neil was the one to bring it up.

"The mystery plane," he said. "Who flies at night, Fletch? Or who would fly at night?"

"You're thinking military," I said.

"Maybe the Unified Government isn't all the way down and out," he suggested.

"Beekman would fly at night," I told him.

"If he didn't have to?"

I didn't have an answer to that. This was a world without navigational aids. Flying at night was, literally, flying blind. Seeing the logic of Neil's suggestion wasn't difficult, but the point of it was still elusive.

"So what do we do?" I asked as we floated south into California, the rising sun creeping higher to our left. "How do we decide our reaction if we hear a plane?"

I thought on that for a moment, and came up with at least a partial answer.

"If I recognize it, we take cover," I said. "That'll be the Cessna Dave and I flew in on."

"Now part of Perkins' air force," Neil quipped.

"He said the same thing," I shared. "So he's going to put it to use."

I could only hope that the man didn't have time to weaponize the light aircraft with mounted machineguns, as he'd hinted at. Neil and I had been strafed from the air before at my Montana Refuge, by a minigun equipped helicopter. That had ended poorly for the attacker, thanks to an expertly aimed shot fired by Grace. We had no backup this time, and facing off against an aerial opponent was something to be avoided at nearly all costs.

"Do you remember the plane from the other night?" Neil asked.

I nodded.

"Just different enough from our Cessna," I said.

"So we hide from that one, too."

"Agreed," I said.

That left one consideration and decision.

"One we don't recognize," I said. "That could be Chris Beekman."

I still thought the pilot from Bandon would be days, if not weeks away, from getting one of the aircraft he'd set off to salvage into the air.

"You don't sound optimistic," Neil observed, zeroing in on my doubt.

"I'm not."

"That would seem to leave us in agreement that anything in the air is a potential threat to be avoided," he suggested.

"Just like anything on terra firma," I agreed.

That conclusion we'd come to cemented one fact that we were already faced with—we were on our own. There would be no help. The cavalry wasn't out there.

It was just us. But, despite the danger of that reality, I wasn't afraid, and neither was my lifelong friend. Whatever lay ahead, we were facing it together. There was an odd satisfaction to that aspect of our situation. Just days ago I could not have dreamed that I'd ever get the chance to have Neil Moore at my side, but he was.

Now all I had to do was get him back to the place we both belonged.

Fourteen

Twenty minutes later the stream flattened out, its waters widened across a shallow delta that had once brimmed with tall aquatic grasses. In my mind's eye I could see it, the memory fueled by countless nature documentaries I'd watched over the years. The area we had floated to would once have teamed with waterfowl, ducks and geese moving from place to place up the west coast, stopping in on what must have been a sanctuary for them.

Now, though, the birds were dead and gone, as was the grass which had hidden them, the latter decayed over time to build the soupy muck our boat had bottomed out on.

"End of the line," I said.

Neil nodded and stood, steadying himself with a wide stance in the relatively stable boat. He looked west, and east.

"I see the tops of some buildings to the northeast," he said. "A half mile at the most."

We were in agricultural country, or what had been, so what Neil saw were likely the remnants of some small town left standing amongst the barren landscape. That it would hold any supplies to sustain us was doubtful. And we needed supplies. Food, in particular. For my friend.

Neil lowered himself and sat in the boat again, his upper half teetering for a moment. The meager rations we'd taken from where we'd been held, and from our pursuer's vehicle, were not enough to sustain him after the self-starvation he'd endured. Weakness still slowed him and dulled his actions. The mere act of standing and sitting again had left him lightheaded. He would not admit that, but he knew that I was fully aware of his condition.

"It's not bad," Neil said.

"Not good, either, though, is it?"

He smiled and shook his head.

"The alternative would be worse," he said.

"Can't argue with that," I agreed, then stood, surveying the once swampy area, bulges of muddy earth poking through the dank waters. "We're heading toward whatever town you saw."

"After we sink this boat," Neil said.

"Exactly."

We gathered our meager gear and slung our rifles and slipped over the edge of the boat into the water. It swallowed us to our waist.

"Just enough to submerge it," I said.

We rocked the boat onto its side and let it fill with water, holding it there until it began to settle beneath the surface. The aluminum craft had no natural buoyancy in its structure. Simply swamping it was enough to send it to the bottom, barely a foot of water covering it.

"If they fly a plane over..." I said.

From the air, in daylight, anyone looking down from above would have a decent chance of spotting the unnatural shape amongst the meandering waters spread across the delta. Especially if they were looking for a boat. The scene they'd left behind across the stream from where the pickup had burst into flame could easily provide the first, and only, clue needed.

"Fletch, let it go," Neil said, reading me like he'd always been able to. "We don't have time to go back. It is what it is."

He was right. But so was I. The reality, though, was that we had only one choice—keep moving.

"Let's get out of this muck," I said.

I began moving toward what appeared to be the edge of the delta, a rise there perfectly dry, the morning breeze kicking wisps of dust just beyond it. Every step was a herculean effort.

"This is like walking through syrup," Neil said.

It was. But a few minutes after we started we reached the edge and climbed from the foul water. Near the top of the rise we stopped and looked out toward what was, indeed, a town. The kind of burg in the middle of nowhere where a couple thousand people had found a way to make a living. Until the blight. Surrounded by miles of farm fields, the bounty of Mother Nature at its doorstep, places like what lay in the near distance were the hardest hit. What they'd always had available, what they believed they could count upon, was the first thing ravaged by the apocalypse.

"We can't head straight in," Neil said.

I saw that his gaze was fixed on the fields that lay between us and the unknown town, an expanse of dusty earth covered by swirls of dried earth shifted by daily winds. Not a living thing had tread across the terrain recently. Possibly not for years. And if we were to do just that...

"We'll leave a bigger mark than where we got the boat," I said, understanding.

Neil looked east, scanning the nearly featureless landscape.

"There's a canal that spills into this," he said, pointing. "I think I see a bridge over it."

A bridge meant a crossing. Likely a road.

"We stay on the bank of the canal to the road, then walk into town," he suggested.

"The canal will give us cover if we need it," I said.

"Let's hope we don't," he added.

This time my friend led off, taking us to where the old irrigation canal began. Now it was simply an avenue for runoff, the waters of the delta backing up into it when the volume was too great. We stayed low, just our head and shoulders above the berm that defined its northern edge. In twenty minutes we reached the bridge and climbed up from the waterway onto a two-lane road, its asphalt surface severely rutted and cracked, huge chucks of blacktop missing, likely washed away by storms over the years. A vehicle would have difficulty navigating the narrow highway at any decent speed. By foot it would be no problem.

But the town was to the north now. We would be backtracking.

"We could just keep going south," I said more than suggested.

Neil looked behind. There was little in that direction. A few buildings, likely farmhouses scattered across the landscape.

"We'd be exposed," my friend pointed out. "If we get into that town we can look for anything useful. Get some rest. Lay up until nightfall."

"Move in the dark," I said, nodding.

We said no more. Once again, Neil took the point. That we were thinking of our movement in such tactical terms was not alien, but it was unexpected. The world had been whittled down to the few of us who'd survived, and I wondered frequently, even before this latest encounter with Perkins, how many remained who had chosen the path of domination over cooperation. Those were the forces that still required us to maintain some tactical order. We were not just two friends strolling along a country highway—we were fighters in enemy lands.

And we would be until we found our way back to Bandon.

* * *

We passed collapsed grain silos and a burned-out ranger station, the remnants of the sign near the highway telling us it serviced the Modoc National Forest. Another sign further on, toppled by years of exposure and neglect, remained readable enough to give the town ahead a name.

"Welcome to Tulelake," I said, reading the lettering.

"Population One Thousand Twenty," Neil said, noting what was written at the bottom of the sign. "I highly doubt that."

"Let's cut across," I said, gesturing to railroad tracks just west of the highway, and to a series of standing warehouses beyond.

This time I led off, crossing a strip of bare earth before reaching the railroad tracks. In two minutes we were walking across large parking lots behind the warehouses, a few wrecked eighteen-wheelers abandoned near the buildings, each resting on flat tires or bare rims.

"This place has been picked clean," Neil said.

"There may be something," I told him. "Our scouting missions have found anything you can think of. Old canned food, whole wine cellars."

"I'll drink to that," Neil said.

We laughed together at that. But only for a few seconds. The sound rising from just north of us ended the brief flourish of joy.

"Car," Neil said.

Neither of us needed prodding. We ran, making our way between two of the warehouses and slipping into an old equipment shed, its plank walls nearing the point of total collapse.

"Just one," I said.

We each took a slice of the pie, Neil covering the west and south, while I kept my AK trained at the opening on the north side of the ramshackle building. Door hanging askew on sagging hinges.

"It's turning," Neil said. "Heading west now."

The vehicle we'd heard had come down the very highway we'd been on just moments before, traveling south until it made a right turn, heading into town. I eased myself closer to the north wall and peered through the space between the old siding, catching sight of what we'd heard as it drove past the first warehouse.

"It's a van," I said.

"And?"

Neil waited for more information. What I had to add wasn't anything close to positive.

"It's turning into the front lot."

We were on the eastern edge of town. The warehouses were the first structures one would see when leaving the highway. That anyone searching for us would start there was not a surprise, but the timing of our arrival with theirs was spectacularly bad luck.

"Only one vehicle?" Neil asked.

"Yeah."

He thought, shaking his head.

"Perkins wouldn't just send one party into town," he said. "There'll be another one on the west side of town."

"They'll work their way through and meet in the middle," I said.

"Unless they spot us first," he said.

We couldn't allow that to happen. If any action was going to happen, we had to initiate it.

"We're in a good spot to ambush," I told Neil.

"We sure as hell are," he agreed. "What do we have left? Four spare mags?"

"That's it," I confirmed. "Shots are going to have to count."

Neil looked to me, and I to him. We'd fired at Perkins' forces as we fled Klamath Falls, but this was different. Here, if it came to that, we would be fighting alongside each other, counting on the other as we had many times in conflict after the blight wiped the rules of civilized behavior away for many.

"Let's see how this plays first," Neil suggested.

I nodded, and we turned again to watch what was coming our way, both of us focused on the van as it entered the parking lot.

Fifteen

The van cruised slowly toward our position and stopped, its engine idling for a moment before it was shut off. The driver's door swung open and a man stepped out, immediately slinging his pistol grip shotgun and lighting a long hand-rolled cigarette. He took a drag and scanned the area casually, as if he had not a care in the world.

"That's Donny," Neil whispered to me.

He'd obviously become acquainted over the years with the survivors who'd coalesced around Earl Perkins. A quick glance toward my friend told me that he held this particular individual in extremely low regard.

"He's an animal," Neil added softly. "He was Perkins' enforcer until he got drunk one day on a stash of booze he came across back in Nevada. That knocked him down a few notches."

"And Bryce stepped up," I said.

Neil nodded, watching with me as Donny left the cigarette dangling in his mouth and thumped the hood of the van with a gloved fist. The side door slid open and three more individuals stepped out, two men and a woman, all armed with AK47s.

"You recognize any of them?" I asked Neil.

"Just the girl," he said. "Her name's Kim, I think. The other guys I'm not sure."

We watched in silence as the three joined Donny at the front of the van. He pointed to several locations. A half-collapsed office in front of the warehouses. A trio of three trailers tipped on their sides.

And the shed where we'd taken cover.

"If they approach, I'll take Donny down," Neil said. "He's an animal, but he knows how to fight."

That meant he knew how to kill.

"I'll cover the others," I said.

The trio from the back of the van began moving toward the trailers which had been knocked on their sides in some wind event, I surmised. Their split back doors were half open, lower section resting on the ground. The group checked each long trailer, none seeming even the slightest bit worried.

"They don't expect to find us," I said.

"Good," Neil said. "Maybe they won't."

If they missed us and then moved into town, clearing it to their satisfaction before heading out, that meant we could, in effect, occupy the area until nightfall. We could search for supplies, futile as that effort might be. Still, it would give a chance to rest and move on.

But that would never happen.

"They're moving our way," I said.

The three had satisfied themselves that the toppled trailers had not provided us with any hiding space and were now walking straight toward the shed in which we'd found cover. It was not the best position we could have moved to, but time wasn't on our side as we'd heard a vehicle approaching. And now the flimsy structure that afforded more concealment than protection was going to be where we would fight from.

"I'm on Donny," Neil said, snugging his AK to a sighted firing stance where he knelt.

The others were mine to deal with. I needed to wait until they were close enough, not only to us, but in proximity to each other. I couldn't afford to be shifting my aim wildly.

"When they reach that tank, I'm firing," I told Neil.

An old propane tank, long emptied of its contents, stood just to the right of our position some twenty yards distant. One of the warehouses sat to the north of it, and the van with Neil's target just to the south. The sight picture would work almost perfectly when they passed in front of the tank. All I had to do was neutralize all of them before they could rake the shed with fire.

"Ready," my friend said.

I didn't have to respond. My first shots would signal him to fire. I waited, watching, picking which person I would take out first.

Kim...

Of the three, she seemed most prepared. Her weapon was held low and ready, finger next to the trigger. She'd had some training somewhere. Possibly, like Sheryl Quincy, she'd been in the military. Or it could be nothing more than the reality of survival in this world. She'd had to fight to stay alive.

I was about to take that from her.

The trio reached the long propane tank and the concrete pad it was mounted to. They crossed in front of it. I let a breath slip past my lips and settled the AKs front sight on the woman I was about to kill.

Then I briefly squeezed the trigger.

The action was quick and effortless. My finger came down on the trigger and then released it, sending a brief burst of automatic fire tearing into the woman who was my first target. She spun and fell, her companions reacting first to flee, turning away from the source of fire, only one managing to bring his weapon up. As I fired again I heard Neil open up, just one quick burst to match mine. The two left in my sight fell, my weapon tracking them to the ground. That was it.

Except it wasn't.

"Dammit!"

I heard my friend curse just an instant before a shower of bullets tore through the slatted wall of the shed just over our heads. My attention shifted instinctively toward the sound of incoming fire and, past Donny's dead body in front of the van, I could just make out muzzle flashes and the silhouette of a figure through the open side door.

One of their group had remained inside.

Neil was the first to return fire, peppering the van with rounds that chipped dark holes in its rusty exterior, shattering the windshield and flattening the right rear tire. I was about to join him in putting rounds on the unexpected target when the whole of my left side erupted in what felt like fire.

"Ahhh!"

My AK whipped upward and was ripped from my grip. I rolled to my right, my left arm and hand pulled tight against my chest as the fire from the van's interior ceased. Neil's shots had found their mark.

"Fletch!"

He glanced toward me, his gaze bulging before he turned his attention again toward the threats we'd just neutralized. I eased my hand away from chest and saw a bloody mess, so much so that it was hard to tell just what had happened, though I knew one thing for certain.

"I'm hit," I said, forcing a calm upon my words.

Neil bolted up from where he'd positioned himself and stepped past me, rushing for the shed's doorway.

"Stay in cover," he said.

He raced out, and through the space between the wall's boards I could see him moving from body to body, checking each, then approaching the van and disappearing into its interior. I turned my attention to my left hand, squeezing the palm with my right, the pressure slowing the flow of blood that was coming from where my ring finger had been.

"Damn..."

I looked to where the AK lay next to me, its barrel bent from the impact of an incoming round which had struck it and then me, severing my finger. The bloody digit lay in two pieces just a few feet away, the wedding ring which had circled it crushed where the bullet had struck. Elaine had had Hannah Morse in Bandon craft it specially for me before our wedding, and now that priceless symbol, and the finger it had proudly worn it, were shattered.

In pain and frustration I kicked at the useless AK, sending it sliding across the small space. We did not live in a world where micro-surgery could replace severed pieces of the human body. Not anymore. Even if that were still a specialty in abundance there was no chance my mangled finger could be reattached.

You've been shot twice...

That thought rose as the wave of pain crested. Yes, I had been shot before. By self-proclaimed Major James Layton in Whitefish. I'd killed him in a final confrontation after a round from his weapon had found me. Now, Neil had eliminated the next person who'd shot me.

"Fletch..."

I looked up and saw my friend just inside the shed. A backpack was slung over one shoulder, and he carried an extra AK, an obvious replacement for the one that had been shot from my hands.

"How bad?"

"A finger," I said, coming to my knees, the wound still bleeding despite the pressure. "Layton gave me worse."

Neil had arrived at my refuge with Grace and her daughter as that wound, in my jaw, had become infected and threatened to end my life. His future wife's nursing background had certainly saved me from an agonizing demise. She wasn't here now, though, to tend to me. No one was.

Except my friend.

"Let me see," Neil said as he knelt next to me, examining the damage before reaching into the backpack. "I grabbed some food and mags from the van. But we're going to have to move. They have a radio. The one who surprised us could have put out a broadcast."

"If they have another group on the west side of town like you said, the gunfire was enough to give us away," I said.

"All the more reason to bandage you up and get out of here," he told me.

He retrieved a long multicolored head and neck wrap from the backpack and wrapped the shemagh around my left hand and pressed a length of it down onto the opening where my ring finger had been.

"Ahhhhh," I winced loudly.

"Life's tough," he said, feigning zero sympathy.

"Yeah, yeah," I reacted, forcing down any further reaction to the pain. "Be tougher."

He finished the quick dressing of my wound and stood, holding a hand down to help me up. Once I was on my feet he handed me the replacement AK. I took it and reached for the backpack.

"You sure you've got that?" he asked, concerned after what I'd just gone through.

"You've had a few crackers and some beans in, what, days?" I pressed him. "Weeks? I'm lighter by a finger."

Neil smiled and let me carry the heavier pack, taking the shoulder bag we'd previously acquired for himself.

"How long do you think we have?" I wondered aloud.

"Let's not find out," he said and hurried out of the shed.

I followed him, glancing down at my hand and the blood already soaking through its wrap. It hurt like hell, but I knew one truth that made the discomfort easier to bear—it could have been worse. Much worse.

Part Three

The Hunted

Sixteen

We backtracked south, leaving the warehouse complex behind, then skirted the edge of town to the west until we found another old irrigation canal, moving away from Tulelake as we hunched low beneath its sloped sides.

Five hundred yards south of the burg's closest structure we heard gunfire.

"They're shooting at shadows," Neil said.

The second patrol had clearly come upon the location of the ambush we'd executed and were likely moving through the warehouses, shooting into every possible hiding space. That didn't demonstrate discipline or anything close to proper tactics, but, in the end, it might not matter. A horde of fanatics firing wildly would easily overwhelm what the two of us could bring to bear.

"As long as they think we're still in town," I said, needing to say no more.

"If they keep thinking that until dark we might have a shot at clearing this area," Neil agreed.

I stumbled slightly, recovering quickly in the shallow depression. No water filled the dry bottom of the canal we were following south. Years of runoff sediment and wind driven dust storms had filled it, reducing its depth by almost half. I readjusted the pack Neil had taken, feeling its contents shift, shapes within pressing against my back. Odd shapes.

"What else did you grab?" I asked.

My friend glanced back at me as he kept pressing forward, staying low.

"A few grenades," he answered. "A road flare. Binoculars. Half empty water bottle."

The water was more useful than the explosive ordnance, I thought. The day was already feeling hot. We were eight hours from sundown and, combining what we had in the shoulder bag and the backpack, we had enough for both of us to have a couple substantial drinks, and that was it. The murky water we might come across ahead if the canal deepened would be a no go without treatment or boiling, neither of which were practical in our situation.

"How's the hand?" Neil asked.

Before I could answer a massive BOOM cracked behind us. We stopped and took cover, pressing our bodies against the sides of the canal as we looked north toward the town we'd just fled. A burst of debris was arcing through the air, slabs of metal and wood hurled outward from an enormous blast, smoke column rising from the unseen point of origin. But we both knew what had just happened.

"They just blew the warehouses," Neil said.

I nodded and got to my feet again, as did he, both of us staying low as we continued on, moving a bit more quickly now. Something had dramatically changed. A dynamic we both realized. Our pursuers were no longer chasing us down to bring us back. Instead, some form of scorched earth policy had been set in motion. That could only happen if word to do so had come down from on high.

From Perkins.

"I think we pissed him off," I said as the canal we'd followed met another, a trickle of water in this deeper trough that tracked southeast.

"You think?" Neil quipped back.

Earl Perkins had gone to extreme lengths to locate and secure the non-existent pathogen BA-412. In both Neil and I he'd believed he could find the answer to his quest for this holy grail. But we'd upset his plans by escaping. And done worse in the process.

We'd made him look as small as his physical stature.

BA-412, if it had existed, might have given him the ability to annihilate the residents of Bandon and take the town for himself, and his people. But our slipping free of his tyrannical grasp had crossed a line which he could not allow to go unpunished. All he was to his followers was a figure who wielded power at the snap of a finger. Destroying us was now a requirement to maintain that aura, that illusion, of power.

This was no longer a pursuit—it was a hunt.

* * *

The network of old irrigation canals ended after we'd followed them south for a few hours, spilling us out into an arid, rocky moonscape, jagged knots of basalt poking up from the reddish earth. It was an ancient lava flow, weathered almost to nothing. We were beyond what had once been farmland and had entered terrain that was disturbingly familiar.

"Remind you of anything?" I asked.

"Like that lovely jaunt we took to Cheyenne?" Neil responded, understanding immediately what I was referencing.

The landscape almost echoed with memories of that hellish trip which had begun with the loss of one of our own, Burke Stovich, and ended with the key to survival in our possession. Here, though, there was no goal other than eluding those coming after us and making our way home.

But home was toward the Pacific, and then north along the coast. One of those points on the compass presented a problem at the moment.

"West doesn't look very doable right here," I said.

Neil looked and saw what I did—the slopes of a mountain range in the distance.

"Mt. Shasta is that way," he said.

That peak, and the smaller mountains near it, were an obstacle we were not prepared to tackle. There would be some way through, I knew. A road, paved or just gravel, some old logging track that we could navigate. But knowing which ones wouldn't simply end where the terrain became impassible was the trick.

"Let's trade the grenades for a map," I suggested.

"And water," Neil added.

We'd drank what we had as the canals neared their end. My friend had also downed some more nuts and dried fruit to boost his energy, which was surprisingly robust considering the condition he'd begun this journey in.

"We'll find some," I told him. "If you have mountains, you'll have springs."

Neil nodded and kept moving, a large wall of old, jagged basalt rising from some ancient fissure off to our left. The feature screened us from the road, but we were still in the open, little along the route we'd been forced to take offering any cover whatsoever.

"Over there," Neil said, pointing to his right. "Tracks."

On a low rise a length of train tracks became visible further away from the lava cliff just east of us. I was instantly reminded of the train I'd ridden with Schiavo and others as we made our way back home from her meeting with the President in Columbus, Ohio. That old diesel beast had been manned by the oddest man I'd met in a long time, Ivan Heckerford. He, like the Marine unit he hauled supplies to, was likely no more than dust on the Kansas prairie where we'd left them.

"Colby, Kansas," I said aloud.

"What's that?"

I smiled as my friend looked back to me, puzzled by my quiet outburst.

"Just a place I've been," I said. "One place of many."

And that began a conversation, a long retelling of all that had transpired since my friend's absence. Mostly it was I who spoke, sharing details of people, and places, and events as we paralleled the train tracks heading south, then split off from them as they crossed the highway we'd purposely avoided. For hours I talked, and for hours he listened, until the day that had seemed so long when we'd fled Tulelake began to show the first hints of ending with a wash of reddish light upon the clouds hovering over the peaks to the west.

"What do you want to do, Fletch?"

We'd stopped just past a collection of rubbled buildings, bits of their blue metal roofs still bright amongst the charred and collapsed structures. It had been some highway maintenance yard, I suspected, a backhoe abandoned near mounds of gravel and crushed stone at one end of the facility's yard.

"Not here," I said, answering the unasked question as to what we should do for the night. "Too close to the highway, and it's the only meager shelter for twenty miles."

We could fashion bits of the wrecked buildings into a lean-to of sorts, though no inclement weather seemed likely to threaten. It would be cold, though, once night came fully, so some protection was preferable to none.

"Keep going south then?" Neil asked.

We'd come a fair distance. Maybe twenty miles. The bleeding had stopped where my finger had been severed, and Neil had gotten some calories into him, but walking just shy of a marathon had taxed us both. More than the fatigue, though, was the thirst. We needed water.

I slung my AK and slipped the pack off, fishing something from within. The binoculars.

"Let's just see what our options are," I said.

The optics Neil had taken from the van were mediocre at best, but it was what we had to work with. We stood on a slight rise in the landscape near the destroyed buildings, and from that spot I began scanning to the east, and the south, and the west, searching for any hint as to our best option for cover as darkness began to settle.

"Anything worth considering?" Neil asked.

There wasn't. But there might be. I zeroed in on that very possibility as I scanned the road as it ran southeast of our position.

"There's a sign," I said, handing the binoculars to my friend so he could look. "Five hundred yards up there. It might be an intersection."

It looked vaguely like a smaller road split off from the highway and traveled west, crossing in front of us. But the sign was most important. It might tell us where we were, or what lay ahead.

"Let's check it out," Neil said.

I waved off his suggestion and slipped back into the pack.

"You stay back and cover," I said. "I'll check the sign. If Perkins' people come rolling up that highway you can hit them before they roll up on me."

"I don't like splitting up," he said. "I did that before and what came after sucked."

"You did what you had to," I said. "Now it's my turn. It's totally exposed out there. We'd both be sitting ducks."

He knew I was right, but still it took him a moment to acknowledge that with a nod.

"Do it quick," Neil said, then he left where we'd stopped and moved toward a position near a flattened building to cover the road to the north.

I didn't hesitate, moving with purpose myself, jogging toward the sign. Every step jolted my body and resonated where my left hand had been violated by a wild round of enemy fire. Along with that pain was the grating dryness in my mouth. It was minor suffering compared to what others had gone through, but it would get worse unless we located a place where some relief could be found.

As I neared the point I'd jogged toward I noticed something I hadn't seen through the binoculars. There wasn't one sign—there were two. The second was bent forward, obscured by the other, and both looked to be just one good winter away from being torn from the posts supporting them. At twenty feet I could make out most of the bottom sign, faded arrows on it pointing west toward recognized symbols for camping and boating. When I stood at it I tipped the upper sign so that it was readable, the weathered lettering clear enough to tell me that this was the way we had to go.

Four minutes later I was back with my friend, breathing hard but excited at what I'd found.

"There's a road going west," I told him. "It goes to a lake."

A lake meant water. Even if we had to find a way to make it safe through boiling, it was more than we had now.

"Close?" Neil asked.

I shook my head.

"Twenty-five miles."

The brief flourish of relief he'd felt waned rapidly.

"We don't have much of a choice," I said.

"I know," Neil agreed, accepting what we had to do. "Does this lake have a name?"

"Medicine Lake," I told him.

"That's either promising or cruel," he said, taking stock of the daylight we had remaining. "We sure aren't making it there tonight."

"Like you said, this place won't work," I reminded my friend.

He looked southwest, where the road would lead us. There were hints of dead woods there, trees which had been decimated by the blight still standing, grey sentinels robbed of their vibrance. They would fall at some point with a strong enough storm, but, for now, they could provide cover.

"Those woods are two miles," Neil said. "Maybe three."

"I'd say so," I agreed.

"We can make that with plenty of light left," he said. "Plenty."

He started walking, taking a course across the open terrain that would intercept the road I'd found. From there we'd follow that to the only cover we felt comfortable with.

There was no talking this time as we walked. No sharing of events. We were both worn out and hurting. Beyond that, though, I was sensing something from Neil that was almost alien—a sense not of defeat, but despair.

It was a hint at best. Just a flicker under his voice and a dulling of his gaze. Part of me wondered if it was less the struggle to get home that lay ahead, and more the reality that he might actually see Bandon again. Might actually have to face the woman he loved, who now loved another. Every step he took was both toward salvation and toward an emotional agony I could not imagine.

My friend was tough. As tough as anyone I'd ever known. But what awaited him beyond the hard miles ahead was more than a test of his mettle. Facing this future that had been made real in his absence could very well crush him.

And, I feared, he knew that.

Seventeen

It was more than a stand of dead trees. It was a campground, with spaces for tents and recreational vehicles, and a small store to provide for those patrons who'd frequented the rustic oasis when leisure activities of the sort were common.

"I see cabins," Neil said, pointing through the trees.

There were at least two that I could make out in the waning light. With them, off to the left about a hundred feet, was a fifth wheel trailer, its side screen door in tatters and flapping in the stiff breeze which had built in the past twenty minutes.

"Let's check the store," I said.

Neil nodded and followed my lead, both of us with weapons ready out of habit. I gripped the forestock of mine with my injured hand, the sharpness of the pain I'd experienced in the previous hours dulled now, a hot throbbing having replaced it. I remembered that sensation as similar to how the wound in my jaw felt, when it turned toward infection. That, though, was nothing I could worry about at the moment. When it became possible I would bear the pain and clean the space where my finger had been.

Now, though, I was focused on our search for supplies and a place to rest for at least part of the night.

"Clear," Neil said as he swept the small front space of the campground store.

I moved past him and stepped behind the counter, its cash register upturned on the floor in some pointless theft long ago. A small office was connected to the sales floor, and I cleared that and a storage closet in under a minute.

"Good back here," I reported as I rejoined my friend.

Surveying the smallish space it was hard to imagine that anything useful would be found. But that supposition was wrong. Neil demonstrated that to me by lifting an old plant pot from where it lay on its side next to the front window. It had likely once held some interior greenery, but now contained only crusted dirt which had dried over the years. He dumped the dusty contents and tapped the steel container.

"Now all we need is some water and something to boil it over," he said.

The former was the issue in the arid landscape. And, with night rapidly descending, heading out to search for a source of water, either some trickling stream or leftover pool of rainwater, was ill advised.

As it was, the sound we heard next ended any thought of leaving the shelter of the old store.

"Airplane," Neil said.

I nodded and listened. We'd discussed the ability to differentiate between the plane I'd come in on, which Perkins now possessed, and the unknown craft which had overflown Klamath Falls in the night, as well as our response to either—hiding. Only an unknown, which could be Chris Beekman out searching for us, would have us take the chance of being seen.

But it was still too soon for any aircraft from Beekman's salvage mission to be in the air. And, as it was, I recognized the sound approaching from the east.

"That's the same as the night flyer," I said.

It was the same plane from just days ago. And it seemed to be coming straight at our location, climbing to match the rise in elevation from where we'd left the highway.

"It's not dark yet," Neil said.

That was both good and bad. It meant that we would be visible if we stepped outside in the waning daylight. But it also meant we might be able to glimpse the aircraft as it neared.

"We need to get a look at it," I said.

"And they might see us doing that," Neil cautioned.

I shook my head and leaned my AK against the old counter.

"We have windows and binoculars," I said. "They're not going to spot us inside from the air at a hundred knots."

My friend understood. He dropped the pack and retrieved the binoculars from it, handing them over and taking a position with me at the side of the store's intact front window. I crouched and brought the cheap glasses up, focusing in on the darkening sky above the dead trees, scanning east and north. As I did, without getting a good look, the aircraft passed nearly overhead.

I looked behind, through the open door past the counter.

"There's a window in that office," I said.

I began to head that way, but my friend stopped me.

"It's turning," he said.

He was right. The receding sound of the small plane's engine changed, shifting slightly south before angling at us once again.

"Get ready," Neil told me.

I crouched next to the window again and aimed the binoculars at the sky above where the aircraft should pass over. Twenty second later it did just that, seeming even lower than before as it gave me a quick glimpse of its familiar underside.

"It's a Cessna," I said. "A One Seventy Two."

The high wing aircraft was a near twin to what Dave Arndt had piloted on our trip to Klamath Falls. But not exact. There was one striking difference.

"And it's grey," I said. "Military grey.'

The plane continued on, heading east, no turn this time to bring it back our way. Whatever it had come for, or to see, it had apparently been satisfied and was returning to where it had come from.

"Military," Neil said, the word partly a question.

"It looked that way," I said.

Like the Marine Osprey which had brought our party home from Kansas, or the helicopters stationed aboard the *Rushmore*, the dull coloring was indicative of the low observability desired by military vehicles. It was impossible to know if some survivor somewhere had simply painted an aircraft to match its military brethren, or simply acquired the abandoned plane and restored it to working condition, or if it did actually belong to a still-functioning military unit. None of those considerations, though, were the most curious part of what we'd just witnessed.

"Two times we get stalked by that thing," Neil said. "Do you believe in coincidences?"

"Not that much," I answered."

We backed away from the window and I took my AK in hand again, suddenly unnerved. By a possibility we'd worried about earlier, but discarded as we moved further from our last encounter with Perkins' people.

"How much light is left do you think?" I asked.

"Twenty minutes," Neil estimated. "Maybe."

I moved toward the door we'd entered through, leaving my friend puzzled.

"What are you doing?"

I stopped and looked back to him, an urgency about me. There was a potential answer out there, for both of us, and we needed to know. Our safety, and our lives, might depend upon it.

"The plane is gone," I said, draping the binocular strap around my neck and bringing my weapon up, throbbing hand supporting the business end of it. "And there's something we've got to see."

"What?"

"If we came all this way for nothing," I said.

Eighteen

Neil joined me as we backtracked through the crumbling woods to the road we'd followed to reach the campground. Where its driveway split off from the road we stopped and looked out at the way we'd travelled to reach that point. The elevation gain positioned us a few hundred feet above the barren landscape we'd crossed, long shadows from the mountains fading into a deepening carpet of darkness. But still it was possible to see. To note landmarks in the distance. The highway. The rubbled collection of buildings near it.

And a faint line drawn across the dusty terrain, first to those collapsed structures, and then toward the road which had led us here.

"Dammit..."

Neil swore and held a hand out. I placed the binoculars in them and he raised them to survey the trail we'd left with nothing more than our boots. But what more was needed in the windswept expanse that was devoid of animals to carve game trails, or people who might hike through the bleak beauty.

"We might as well have drawn a map," Neil said.

"That plane wasn't theirs, though," I reminded him.

He lowered the binoculars and handed them back.

"We don't know who they are," he said. "Or who they represent."

Something had drawn that aircraft to Klamath Falls, and then to where we had come. But its purpose was not anything we could worry about at the moment. We had bigger problems, literally, on the horizon.

"Fletch..."

"I see it."

Lights. Lights that were moving along the road to the north. A collection of vehicles heading south.

Heading toward us.

"They can't know we're here," Neil said. "They can't see that trail from where they are."

They were maybe seven or eight miles distant. Spotlights from the caravan were sweeping the open fields to the left and right of the highway.

"That's not just a couple search parties," Neil said.

"No," I agreed.

It was clear from what we were seeing that Perkins had committed all of his resources to hunt us down in this direction. Our initial foray south had planted in his head that we were going to continue in that direction. We'd swung west now in search of water, but would they?

"They're just groping," Neil said. "Hoping to catch sight of us."

"Yeah, well they're groping awful close," I told my friend.

We backed up a bit and crouched next to a small knot of splintered fir trees, using the dead stand as cover. There was almost no chance we could be spotted by them yet, but that was not as comforting as it should be.

"So now we have Perkins and some rogue military aircraft zeroing in on us," Neil said. "I guess we pissed in everyone's cornflakes."

The aircraft was still an unknown, which, in our eyes, made it a threat until we could confirm otherwise. The force moving south along the highway was a definite known. One that we had to steer clear of.

It took the motorized posse ten minutes to reach the old maintenance station, nearly full darkness spread across the landscape now. The convoy stopped for a few minutes, flashlight beams sweeping the collapsed buildings.

"They're not shooting," Neil observed.

The patrol which had raced to where we'd ambushed their fellow fighters at the warehouse complex had fired wildly, performing an act of reconnaissance by gunfire. This much larger group wasn't doing anything of the sort. To both of us, that meant one thing.

"Perkins is with them," I said.

Neil nodded. For all the idiocy that the man possessed, he had moved an entire population from Yuma to Klamath Falls. That required force, but also planning.

"He's listening to Sheryl and Bryce," Neil said.

"Why Bryce?"

Sheryl Quincy had been a soldier before shedding that honor to become a turncoat in service of the Unified Government. She'd had training in combat tactics. But what made Perkins' right-hand man as capable in Neil's estimation?

"He was a PJ," my friend said. "Air Force Para Rescue. Badass dudes. They can kill you or save your life—their choice."

Neil looked to me as I processed what he had just shared.

"Judge him for joining Perkins," he said. "Not for turning his back on the government that left all but a few elites to fend for themselves."

Once more he was reading me, as no one else could. We couldn't have been closer than if we'd been born brothers. What we'd faced before, and what we were facing now, had only solidified that bond.

"He still threw in with a maniac," I reminded my friend.

"I'm just saying his reason for fighting is valid to him," Neil explained. "And he'll fight like hell. I can promise you that."

"So will we," I said.

Neil nodded and we both looked down toward the convoy again. It was still stopped at the rubbled facility along the highway, a careful search being carried out. The professionalism we were witnessing from a distance was unsettling. Particularly when we saw a small unit split from the main force and move southwest across the open fields, their flashlights arcing back and forth across the darkness. Searching.

"Damn," I said.

Hardly a second after my explanation the searchers stopped. A moment later more fighters from the main force moved quickly toward them. They'd found something.

Our trail.

"How the hell did they know to look out there?" I wondered aloud.

"We left traces," Neil said. "And they're motivated."

We could only be so careful in our flight from captivity. When one was on the run they couldn't brush away every track they'd left behind. And we clearly hadn't.

"They're going to be coming," I said.

Neil stood next to the tree where we'd taken cover.

"Let's not wait for them," he said.

We turned and moved back through the dead trees to the RV campground. I'd hoped there would be time to scavenge from the few cabins on site, and the long-abandoned trailers and motorhomes. That wasn't to be.

"What's our move here?" Neil asked.

I didn't have to think long on his question as we hurried past the small campground store and toward the area where the rustic cabins had been sited.

"Keep moving in the direction of the lake," I said. "But we stay south of the road heading up there. In the trees if we can."

"Right on," Neil agreed.

If we could follow that plan, that course, it would, hopefully, hide any tracks we left from easy observation, from either the ground or the air. That didn't take into consideration our need for water, and my friend's still weakened state.

None of that mattered, though. Not now. We simply had to put distance between us and Earl Perkins until we were convinced it was safe to focus our energy on getting home. As it was now, we were running for our lives.

Nineteen

It took us three hours to cover four miles, heading almost due south before we swung west into a grey forest that the road to Medicine Lake cut through. Almost as soon as we entered the woods we heard it.

Water.

It came from a point in the darkness off to our left, even further from the winding road that we'd avoided. Navigating the sloping terrain to reach the source of the sound sent each of us falling several times. One such stumble smashed my wounded hand against the snapped stump of a fallen fir.

"Ahhh..."

I didn't scream, but I couldn't completely staunch the reaction to the pain.

"You all right?"

Neil stopped and came to me, backtracking a few yards to where I'd come to sit against the remnants of the tree. I clutched my left hand against my chest, making a fist that felt sickeningly incomplete with a missing finger.

"Let me see," Neil said.

He took my hand and unwrapped the shemagh which had served as a makeshift bandage since our firefight in Tulelake. In the forested darkness it was nearly impossible to see, even close up, but my friend only took a few seconds to examine my hand before wrapping it again, tighter this time.

"It's bleeding again," he said.

"I can tell," I told him. "And..."

He stood and held his weapon in one hand, holding the other down to help me up.

"A nice little infection starting," he said.

I took his hand and stood with help, planting my feet carefully on the uneven slope. The sound of water was close, coming from maybe fifty feet distant. We both needed to hydrate. Badly. Dealing with my hand would have to wait.

"I'll clean it off after we tank up," I said.

Neil gave me a solid slap on the shoulder and turned, heading out with me on his heels. In two minutes we came around a bulge in the easing terrain and saw what we'd come for.

A stream.

"Spring or runoff?" Neil wondered aloud.

"Does it matter?"

He shook his head. In a perfect situation we'd boil any water we came upon that wasn't released by an underground spring in the vicinity. Runoff could contain any number of nasty particles, though worrying about things like giardia had gone out with the last wild animal who might take a dump and contaminate lakes and rivers. Rotting bodies had, for a time, been a concern. But those times were mostly past.

"I think it's runoff," I said.

"Makes sense if there's a lake up there," he agreed.

We shed our gear and lay our AKs on the ground then crouched next to the stream and cupped drinks from the dark water in our hands and drank. And drank. After a few minutes Neil filled the few water containers we had in the pack and the shoulder bag while I unwrapped my hand and plunged it into the cold water, the contact stinging initially before shifting toward a comfortable numbness. It was odd looking down at the shadowy appendage and seeing a part missing. I could just make out an area of redness which did, as my friend suggested, look like the beginnings of an infection, as well as bruising and swelling of the adjacent fingers.

"It's gonna look weird when you flip someone off," Neil commented.

I lifted my right hand momentarily and gave him the middle finger.

"Good thing you have a spare," he said.

Finished with caring for my wound I bandaged it again and sat back against a large rock near the stream. Aside from the gentle babbling of the waters, it was silent. Even through that hushed trickle distant sounds would be apparent.

But we heard none.

"There's been nothing on the road," I said.

"No vehicles, you mean," Neil corrected me.

We were just under a mile from the strip of asphalt winding up into the mountains toward Medicine Lake. In these conditions, at that distance, we should have heard the rumble of the convoy's trucks and cars pursuing us, but we hadn't.

"They'll be coming," Neil assured me. "They found our tracks. They know we're close. Perkins can smell us. He can taste it, you know."

I did know. Now that his plan had shifted from exploiting us to killing us, he would be imagining the satisfaction of that very end result. He'd be picturing the moment in his mind.

"You think they're on foot?" I asked my friend.

"We're on foot," he reminded me.

It was possible Perkins had ordered his people to leave the vehicles behind so as not to alert us. Or they could just be waiting where they'd found our tracks.

Or, or, or...

We were in the dark literally and figuratively. One of those we could at least use to our advantage for the time being.

"We should rest here," I said.

Neil surveyed the dim spot we'd stopped for a much-needed drink. It was as isolated as any location we'd passed and was shielded from view from all sides. The rocky ground we'd crossed to reach the stream would not show any tracks we might have left, though both of us had been more aware of doing so since realizing how easily we'd been located near the campground.

"So we're moving in daylight now," he said, only half accepting of the implication of stopping for the night.

"If we stay in the woods it's good cover," I said.

He considered that for a moment then nodded. We slipped back into a routine that was both distant and familiar at the same time, one of us taking the first shift awake while the other slept. In places far different than this we had adopted the same security procedures to avoid being ambushed, and we had survived, as we were now. Neil settled in on the ground behind a pile of boulders and drifted off to sleep within minutes. His body needed recharging more than mine, and in the dark, cool stillness I sat, silent, listening.

I heard nothing but the stream babbling down the mountain that, in the morning, we would begin climbing again.

Twenty

Six hours after we woke and began moving west again, I heard something.

"That's just the water," Neil told me when I'd directed his attention to the sound.

He could have been right in some respects. The stream still ran off to our left, trickling down from the still distant lake. But I did not hear water babbling along.

"I heard splashing, Neil," I said.

We stopped and spread out, each of us taking a knee a dozen yards apart in the old grey woods. The terrain had flattened out, plateauing at the elevation where Medicine Lake was likely situated somewhere ahead. Without a map we had no sure way of knowing its exact location, relying instead on the stream to guide us there so that the road could be avoided.

After a few minutes of listening Neil looked to me and shook his head. I nodded and we rose again, coming back together to continue our way forward.

"I don't know what it was," I told my friend, my voice hushed.

"A piece of deadfall falling into the water," he suggested.

That was possible. It made more sense than any of the nefarious scenarios I could imagine, where Perkins' people would have found a way to get ahead of us and were, as we pressed on, surrounding us near the stream.

Twenty minutes later, though, there was no sign of any pursuer. No sign of any danger at all.

Until there was.

The sound this time was not some nebulous sloshing of water. It was the straining rumble of a diesel engine off to our right in the direction of the road. A vehicle was chugging its way up the mountain. It was climbing slowly but wasn't stopping.

"Just one," I said as Neil and I both shifted to full cover behind a pair of trees.

"Where are the rest?" he wondered aloud.

"We need to see what it is," I said.

It was a risk, closing the distance we'd kept from the road, but without doing so we would be advancing in the blind. For all we knew the creeping vehicle could be dropping groups of fighters as it continued on. Groups that could be setting up to swarm us once we were spotted.

"All right," Neil agreed, no fervor about him. "But we stay well clear of being exposed."

I nodded and we started moving again, shifting course to the northwest, aiming at a point which, were we to continue on our chosen heading, would intersect the road a quarter mile away. Traversing rises and falls in the terrain we finally reached a point just past the crest of a hill bulging from the mountain's east slope. From that vantage point, as we went to ground and shielded ourselves behind a dense knot of fallen trees, we were able to see the road maybe forty yards through the woods.

"Still coming," Neil said.

The vehicle, sounding more like a truck now that we'd closed the distance, hadn't yet reached the sliver of the road we could see. But it was close. I brought my AK up and kept it at the ready. From the prone position we could unleash a first volley of fire unimpeded, if that became necessary.

I hoped it wouldn't.

"There," I said.

Neil tracked my gaze to the right, the nose of the flatbed just coming into view. We immediately realized why it was moving so slowly, more than just the incline responsible. On its back, in the chair bolted to the cargo bed, Perkins sat, surveying the landscape as a dozen of his fighters walked alongside.

"Twelve on each side," Neil said quietly.

Two dozen enemy to deal with if all hell broke loose. But it was more than what we saw pacing the truck. Sheryl Quincy sat next to Perkins, cross-legged on the flatbed, facing backward, a SAW resting on her lap. The squad automatic weapon, if brought to bear, could rain a steady stream of lead hell upon us, the box magazine attached to it holding at least a hundred rounds. That one weapon alone outgunned us, and when combined with armada Perkins had brought with him...

"Let's give them a wider berth," I said.

"Much," Neil said.

We crawled slowly backward once the truck and its phalanx of fighters had passed, reversing until we were on the other side of the low crest, fully shielded from view now.

"That's not all of them," Neil said once we were in the clear. "There were at least four sets of headlights on the highway last night."

I nodded. Perkins had divided his force into smaller, yet still formidable units, spreading out from the tracks we'd left behind. How many were in our immediate vicinity was impossible to know.

"You still think that splash was a branch falling into the water?" I asked my friend.

He didn't have an answer, and neither did I. Worse still, though, was the reality we faced—we *had* to move. And somewhere out there we could find ourselves in an ambush like the one we'd sprung on Perkins' people at the warehouses.

"There's every chance it was just that," Neil said. "But we act like it wasn't."

For five minutes we held our position, listening until the sound of the truck was no more. Then we waited ten minutes more, hearing nothing but the stream rustling softly to the south.

"I'll take the lead," I said.

We stood and began moving, Neil positioning himself ten yards behind me as I set our course to the west, maneuvering us around terrain obstacles and stopping short of old logging roads which cut across our path. We would hold position and survey those before quickly crossing, checking for signs that the truck we'd seen, or any vehicle, had recently passed. There were none.

We pressed forward, keeping the stream off to our left, taking brief breaks as the afternoon crept toward evening, the lake somewhere ahead of us through the crumbling woods.

splash...splash...splash

I stepped behind a tree and froze, looking back to Neil, who'd taken a similar position and gave me a quick nod. He'd heard it, too, this time. And it was no branch falling. It was the sound of running through water.

But as soon as it was there, the sound was gone. Again. Neil moved up, setting himself off to my left, closer to the stream.

"It sounded like it was moving away from us," he said. "Upstream."

I agreed. Whoever had sloshed through the babbling water was moving in the same direction we were, roughly toward the lake which was almost certainly the source of the flow.

"It's not a well-set ambush," I said.

"Maybe because it's not that," Neil said. "But it could be drawing us into one."

"Bait," I said.

Perkins had used the tactic before, luring Dave Arndt and me to land and check out a patch of green woods that were as fake and dead as those that surrounded them. A similar approach could be in play here.

But something told me that suspicion was off base.

"Why not just wait for us ahead if they know enough to bait us?" I asked. "The sound could just as easily drive us off."

Neil considered that for a moment, nodding agreement.

"Then who is it?"

"One way to know," I said.

We stepped from behind the trees and resumed our push west, the slope easing as the wooded land around us flattened out. I shifted our course closer to the stream as it cut a depression in the terrain, seeking its uneven banks as a source of cover. Once we reached it one of the questions we'd had about the splashing was answered.

"Tracks," I said.

Neil moved cautiously forward and crouched next to me, looking to where I was pointing.

"You've gotta be kidding me," he said.

But there was no mistaking what we were seeing.

"There's a dog out here," I said.

Twenty One

We'd both grown up around enough wildlife, both domesticated and otherwise, to recognize what we were seeing and differentiate it from natural, if unlikely, alternatives.

"Not coyote," Neil said. "They died out long ago."

The scavenging predators had seen their place on the food chain wiped out soon after the last bit of carrion, beast or human, had been devoured. Their presence was not an option.

"If there's a dog," I said.

"Then there are people keeping it alive," I completed his thought.

Neil scanned the stream ahead, the narrow waterway deep in shadow. We had a couple hours of light left at best. There'd been no repeat appearance by the truck or any other vehicle, and though we wanted to assume that meant Perkins and his fighters were not nearby, we could take no such assurance from the absence of signs.

Mixed among that reality, though, was another worry.

"We heard whosever dog this is twice now," I reminded my friend. "Miles apart."

"You think they're tracking us?"

"I think we have more company than just Perkins," I said.

* * *

We heard no more splashing but did see an abundance of paw prints along the damp bank of the stream. The animal was a good size and was definitely moving west, seemingly just ahead of us.

Shortly we believed we understood why that was.

"Building," I said.

Neil came forward again where I'd stopped along the crest of the stream bank and looked at what I had spotted. It was a cabin, situated in the dense woods, the dead trees nearest the structure having been obviously cut down to prevent deadfall from crushing the modest structure. The stream passed to the south of the almost quaint home, some thirty yards away, and beyond the log structure an outhouse sat, a path worn in the earth between it and the main building.

"That looks maintained," Neil observed.

"Someone lives there," I agreed.

It was not abandoned. Just the opposite, in fact. The windows were intact, shades behind each drawn, no light bleeding out. There was a chimney, but no smoke curled skyward from it. Yes, someone was in there, but they were taking pains to be unseen.

To be left alone.

"What do you think, Fletch?"

"I'm not sure they'd appreciate a pair of armed strangers knocking," I said.

A moment later any thought of approaching the cabin to introduce ourselves was made moot as a beautiful Doberman Pinscher appeared from the back side of the building and trotted our way.

"We've been spotted," Neil said.

I brought my weapon up, ready to fire upon the dog should it attack. Quickly, though, my concern eased somewhat, as the animal was not running toward us, its demeanor stoic but not aggressive.

And, we both saw, it held something in its mouth—a rolled up piece of paper.

"It's playing messenger," Neil said.

The Doberman, a male we could now see as it neared our position, stopped just a few feet away and relaxed its jaw, letting the paper fall to the ground near the stream bank.

"Good boy," I said.

The dog stared at me for a moment, then turned and ran back toward the cabin, disappearing behind it. Neil reached out and took the note in hand, unrolling it to read what was within.

"Do not approach our house. Leave the area. We only want to live in peace but we will defend ourselves. We have before."

My friend handed the note over after reading it. It was simple and to the point, telling in only a few respects.

"More than one in there," I said. "Could be two or ten."

"Too small," Neil said. "Not ten."

I scanned the area in the waning light. The backwoods cabin was isolated, no road passing within a half mile, it seemed. Whoever had built it had done so with a purpose in mind. Maybe this very purpose—to ride out some apocalyptic catastrophe.

"Let's leave them be," Neil said, crumpling the note and burying it under a rock. "We don't need another fight and they don't seem eager to have one."

I couldn't argue with his logic, nor with his consideration toward the unknown individuals beyond the shaded windows. Despite that, there was the draw toward some understanding of how it was possible that an isolated group of people, with a dog, had survived when so many had perished. This was not a large community like Bandon, with a collection of resources and knowledge. It was more like my refuge north of Whitefish where I'd bugged out when the proverbial crap began to hit the fan.

But simply wanting to know something did not guarantee that answers would come. It was best, as my friend suggested, that we get moving and keep moving.

Neil stood and raised a hand in full view of the cabin, then he turned and began backtracking. I followed. We retraced our steps along the stream, then, a few hundred yards back, turned north before reaching the road that should be off to our right. With less than an hour of light left we passed the point where the cabin would be to our left and pressed on toward the lake, a wide field of blowdown slowing our progress a half hour later.

"How are you doing?" I asked my friend as he scrambled slowly over the stacks of decaying pines and firs.

"The needle's on E," he told me.

"Stop on the far side of this mess?"

Neil nodded at my suggestion, the decision to make some sort of camp made. As it turned out, that wasn't to be.

"Plane," I said, hearing the sound rise from the east, approaching from the direction we'd traveled.

Neil rolled over a log and pressed himself as far underneath it as he could. I did the same, the cover meager at best. We were just yards apart, eyeing each other through the space beneath a toppled tree.

"That's not the same plane," Neil said.

I shook my head. It wasn't. Instead, it was familiar.

"That's the plane we came in on," I told him.

"You're sure?"

"Unless there's another one like it in the area, yes," I said.

That meant that Perkins had finally gotten the captured plane into the air and was pressing it into service looking for us.

"This is not a good position," Neil commented, trying in vain to burrow his body and gear deeper under the dead tree.

He was right. And that fact was about to work against us.

"He's descending," I said.

The Cessna was slowing, its altitude changing as it neared the field of blowdown. It passed over then circled the area in a wide arc before seeming to settle into an orbit directly above us.

"He might have us," I said.

"Just stay still," Neil said. "It's dark."

For a few minutes the plane remained over us before shifting its position to the east and south, orbiting a landmark we'd left behind.

"It's got the house," I said.

"Just don't move," Neil reminded me. "They have night vision and you can bet those optics are on that plane."

I knew he was right. An observer, maybe more than one, would be scanning the landscape below, searching for anything that didn't belong, like a house. Or us.

"It's backing off," Neil said.

We both eased our heads up and looked east toward the fading sound, the white plane gleaming in the last rays of the setting sun as it flew away from us.

"Let's move," Neil said. "Into the trees then due north."

"That's away from the lake," I said.

"They expect us to be heading there for water," Neil said as we began crawling over log after log, the line of still standing woods fifty yards away. "We've got enough in bottles for a day or two."

"You're right," I said, following fast, both of us fueled by adrenalin now.

We reached the cover of the woods and, once we were fifty yards beyond the clearing, we swung right, jogging north, trying to put some distance between us and where we might have been spotted.

We weren't the only ones who might have been spotted, however.

"Neil," I said, stopping.

My friend halted and looked back to me, breathing hard.

"What?"

"We have to go back," I told him.

"Fletch, what are you talking about?"

"I'm talking about doing what's right."

Neil took a few steps and stopped, facing me from just a foot away. He stabbed a finger past me, pointing in the direction we'd just come from.

"Perkins may just have his entire force swarming back there any minute," he warned me.

"We won't be there," I said. "But someone will."

Part Four

Enemies and Friends

Twenty Two

"The people in the cabin?" Neil challenged me.

I nodded.

"The people who told us to leave them alone," he recounted. "Who wanted us gone."

"We just led a maniac and his followers to them," I told my friend. "That plane may not have spotted us, but it sure as hell spotted that cabin."

Neil couldn't counter that statement, but he still seemed reluctant to venture back to where there would almost certainly be a fight. That wasn't the Neil Moore I knew, or had known. But enough time had passed, and enough had transpired that my friend had changed. If not in total, then by some noticeable degree. Noticeable to me.

"You want to get home," I said. "I know that. I—"

"No, Fletch! You don't know! You CAN'T know! You can't know what I've been through, what Perkins did to me, and you damn sure can't know how much I just want to...how much she..."

His burst of rage faded quickly away as his diatribe shifted toward thoughts of her. Of Grace. The woman he'd loved, and now lost to another.

"You can't know," he repeated, his head bowing. "You..."

I stepped toward my friend and pulled him close with one arm, my wounded hand pressed against his back as he wept quietly. I'd never seen such a flood of emotion burst from him. But, as he'd stated, I couldn't know what he was feeling, nor how much he was hurting. In his mind I imagine he saw some reunion in Bandon with Grace, and Krista, and Brandon. He might even allow some fantasy to rise where they could put back together what had existed before he died.

"I just want to see her, Fletch," he said as he eased back from me, dragging a sleeve across his face. "I want to hold Brandon and Krista. I want things to...feel like they used to, even if that's only for a minute or two. That's all I want."

I nodded, understanding as much as I could, which wasn't nearly enough to let me know what that possibility meant to him.

"We'll get there," I said.

Neil looked to me, then looked behind, through the trees in the direction of the house some two miles distant now.

"We have to warn them," Neil said, accepting the reality of our situation. "Those people are going to pay the price for us stumbling upon them."

"We have time," I said. "But we need to move now."

I glanced up through the decaying trees at the greying sky, storm clouds swirling in the near distance. Mother Nature was bearing down on us.

As was Earl Perkins.

* * *

It took us ninety minutes to reach the backwoods cabin, avoiding the blowdown clearing as night settled fully upon the landscape. When we were within a hundred feet of it a pair of red laser dots appeared on each of our chests. Our weapons were already slung, and we raised our hands.

"We're not a threat," I said loudly, chancing revealing our position to any of Perkins' people who, however unlikely, might be in earshot. "But we have a warning for you."

The laser dots held steady, dancing only slightly, each marking the spot where rifle rounds would tear into us should those in the cabin decide to fire. No response came. No verbal response, that is.

"The dog's back," Neil said quietly.

Resolving through the darkness, the silent beast walked toward us, its black coat shimmering like a moving shadow. It stopped twenty feet away and stared at us, making no move.

"Please," I shouted. "You have to believe us."

"Why?"

The question came from behind us and to the left. We turned slowly and saw just the silhouette of a man standing next to a tree, a pump shotgun in hand, the muzzle pointed at us.

"We don't have any reason to lie to you," I said.

The man took a few steps toward us, revealing more of himself in the thin moonlight that filtered through the threatening clouds above, the first cool sprinkles beginning to peck at my cheeks.

"You have every reason to lie to me," the man countered. "If you'd like I can show you the graves of a few others who lied to try and take what we have."

"That's not necessary," I said.

He was not hard, but was hardened. The beard he wore was neatly trimmed, and on his left hand where it gripped the shotgun's pump I noticed the brief glimmer of a ring. A wedding ring.

We hadn't intruded upon some group of survivors— we'd stumbled upon a family.

"We told you to leave," he said.

"We can't," I said.

He raised the shotgun and pointed it at me. Neil moved quickly, bringing his AK up. The dog began to advance, preparing to launch itself at my friend.

"STOP!"

Another voice cut through the darkness. A woman's voice this time. The man, as surprised as we were, looked toward it as we did. Within seconds a woman in her thirties emerged from the shadows, the laser sight of her M4 still fixed on Neil's chest. She approached and stopped next to the dog, which had heeded her command before going fully into attack mode.

"Just, please," the woman said, her gaze shifting between the man who was, presumably, her husband and us. "No killing. No more. Please."

Her husband looked back to me and waited. Neil lowered his weapon first, followed by the man.

"You said something about a warning," the woman said.

"Yes," I confirmed.

"What kind of warning?" she asked.

"Marcia," her husband said, admonishing her for entertaining what we were saying.

"Steven, we can listen," she said.

"I'm Eric Fletcher," I said. "This is Neil Moore. We're from Bandon on the Oregon coast. There's an entire town of survivors there. We have the cure for the blight, seeds that grow, trees, fruits and vegetables. There's livestock."

"None of that sounds like a warning," Steven said. "It does sound like a tall tale, however."

"We're trying to get back there," Neil said. "But the man who was holding us captive isn't keen on letting that happen. He has a good-sized force out looking for us on this mountain. And there's every chance one of his aircraft spotted your cabin a while ago, just before sundown."

Worry bloomed on Marcia's face and she looked to her husband.

"Don't listen to them," Steven told her.

I glanced off into the darkness toward the north.

"There's a road that way," I said. "He had a truck running up there today. I'm guessing you had to hear that."

"We did," Marcia confirmed.

"Marcia!"

She lowered her M4, its aimpoint no longer on Neil's chest. The other laser dot remained on mine.

"Steven, not everyone is a danger. Not everyone is out to hurt us."

"That's not a chance we can take," he said.

"Actually, it's a chance you have to take," I told him. "Because if you don't listen to us you're going to be annihilated. The man who's after us, his name is Earl Perkins, and you're either on his side or you're dead."

Steven didn't respond to that fact I'd shared. We didn't need him to believe it was true, only that it could be. That way he would be more likely to accept that Perkins was more of a threat to him and his family than we could ever be.

"Eric, Neil," Steven said, lowering his shotgun. "Let's get inside before the sky opens up."

Twenty Three

We entered the dim cabin and left our rifles just inside the door, which closed and locked behind us. Steven had instructed us to do so as we approached his family's remote home. A single small candle burned at the center of a rectangular gathering table at the front room's center, with four chairs spaced around it. Two doors led from the space, one on each side of the cold stone hearth, presumably accessing bedrooms and some sort of kitchen at the back of the house.

"Have a seat," Steven said as he moved to the far side of the table with his wife. "Go ahead."

She'd put her M4 in a rough wooden rack next to the fireplace, but he still held his shotgun. It wasn't pointed at us anymore, but it didn't need to be to send a signal—we weren't fully trusted and likely never would be.

Neil and I sat at the table and Marcia lit a larger candle after making sure that the room's blackout shades fully covered the windows. The tripling of light in the space revealed more, and less. There was little in the way of hominess. No pictures or décor to mention. It was impersonal. Even cold. And from that I realized something I suspected our reluctant host didn't want known.

"You have more cabins," I said. "More hideouts."

Marcia looked to her husband, then to me, wary and surprised all at once.

"How can you know that?" she pressed me.

I didn't really need to answer. I simply needed to soak in the look Steven was giving me. With the simple observation I offered I demonstrated to him that whatever plans he and his wife had carefully crafted they were not entirely sufficient to stand against all threats.

"You think this Perkins fellow will find us if we move to another location," Steven said.

"Until he finds us he'll leave scorched earth," Neil said.

Steven considered that for a moment.

"The smart thing might be for me to hand you both over to him," the man said.

It wasn't bluff, nor was it bluster. The words were spoken by a man confronted with a situation which was testing the necessities of his existence—protecting his family and honoring his personal values.

"We're not going to do that," Marcia told me, fixing on her husband next. "We're *not* going to do that."

Steven stood silent for a moment, then lowered his shotgun and let it lean against the hearth. He sat, and Marcia joined him at the table, placing her hand over his as they faced us.

"No matter what happens you can't stay with us," Steven said. "I just want that to be clear. We put aside nine million calories."

"More than," Marcia corrected him. "Nine and a half million. Stored in a safe spot nearby. Enough for four people at twenty-five-hundred calories a day for ten years. And Willow's needs."

"And you didn't plan on any extra for strangers," I said.

"No we did not," Steven confirmed. "Just us and our dog."

I noticed right then that the Doberman we'd encountered multiple times was not with us.

"Where is your dog?" I asked.

"Willow's out doing his job," Steven said.

"Steven trained him," Marcia shared proudly, squeezing her husband's hand. "He's our lookout. He'll roam all over listening and watching and smelling."

I understood, even if what she was describing seemed slightly farfetched.

"Willow's your tripwire," I said.

"In essence," Steven confirmed. "That's how we knew you were coming."

"Trained him not to bark," Neil said. "That's some serious conditioning. He doesn't give himself away. Just comes back and alerts you, I imagine."

"Something like that," Steven confirmed. "Except the silence. You can't train the bark out of a dog."

"Steven was a veterinarian," Marcia shared. "Is a veterinarian."

She didn't have to explain the particulars of why Neil had been wrong about that aspect of the Doberman's performance.

"You debarked him," I said.

"The preferred term is devoiced," Steven corrected me.

The conversation quieted for a moment, the storm building outside, rain drumming on the heavy roof above.

"You've got a nice setup here," my friend told Steven and Marcia. "Preparations. Isolation. And we've seen a lot since the blight hit. But something else is about to hit, and all the calories you've squirreled away won't stop it. Neither will a shotgun and an AR."

"That group that passed by a while back," Marcia reminded him before looking to me. "There were hundreds of them heading north. Is that who you're talking about?"

It had to be, I knew. No other substantial group of survivors could exist now. Not in this area.

"Four hundred," I said. "They came from Yuma to destroy the town I'm from."

I felt Neil's gaze shift my way.

"The town that we're from," I corrected myself.

Steven looked at us both for a moment, a stoic sadness about him. We'd brought a threat to him and his family without ever wanting or intending to.

"Timothy, Penny," the man said, loud enough to be heard in the back of the house. "Come here."

A moment later a young girl came through the doorway to the right of the hearth, followed by an older boy, an M4 with laser sight slung across his chest. Both eyed us warily, much like their pet and protector had.

"This is our daughter, Penny," Marcia said, brushing her little girl's blonde locks off her face. "She's six. And this is Timothy."

"I'm ten," the boy said before his mother could. "Almost eleven."

"His birthday is next month," Martha said, smiling. "On the eighth."

"It's nice to meet you," I said. "I'm Eric."

"I'm Neil. Very pleased to meet you both."

Neither child said anything in response to our greeting. That didn't surprise me. We were likely among the very few people other than their parents they'd seen in years, and certainly for the little girl the blighted world was all she had known.

"I have a little girl," I said, fixing my attention on Penny. "She's younger than you."

The tiniest smile flashed on the child's face, then she nuzzled up close to her mother's shoulder.

"You have a steady aim," Neil said, addressing Timothy.

"My aim was on him," the boy said sharply, nodding toward me. "Not you."

"Timothy," Steven said, gently admonishing his son for the hint of rudeness in his tone. "Put your rifle in the rack and take your sister in the back to play."

Penny shifted from her mother and looked up to her father.

"Can we light a candle?" she asked him.

He smiled, her question, her simple presence, softening nearly all about him for that moment.

"A little one," Steven told her. "Timothy, a little light, okay? Make sure the shades are drawn tight."

The boy slipped his M4 into the rack next to his mother's rifle and nodded, taking his sister by the hand and leading her from the front room. A moment later a lighter clicked and a soft glow built in the doorway behind Steven.

"You've been here since it all began?" I asked, flexing my left hand and adjusting the makeshift bandage.

"You're hurt," Marcia said before either of them could answer.

"Lost a finger," I said. "I can manage without it."

Steven reached across the table and waited for me to present my hand. I hesitated only briefly, then let him have a look. He unwrapped the bandage and eyed the bloody wound.

"He was shot," Neil explained.

"Hopefully you gave better than you received," Steven said, taking the candle in hand and using it to illuminate the space where my ring finger had been.

"We did," Neil assured him.

"The people who are after you did this?" Marcia asked. "The ones who you say are coming?"

"Yes," I answered.

Steven looked to me, then to Neil, and finally to his wife.

"I'm used to working on paws," he said. "But I might be able to tidy this wound up a bit."

"I'll get your medical kit," Marcia said, standing.

"The trauma kit with sutures," Steven told her, looking back to us. "And a meal please, for our friends."

Marcia smiled, one of the truest smiles I'd seen. It was the joy of a person who was welcoming guests into her home, however unexpected they might be. It was the look of earnest hospitality.

"Of course," Marcia said, then disappeared through the doorway to the left of the hearth.

* * *

A few minutes later, after a few strategic lidocaine injections in my battered left hand, Steven began cleaning the wound, carefully trimming away excess skin that remained after my finger was ripped away. Behind him, in the kitchen where soft light glowed, Neil had joined Marcia as she readied food for us.

"You never answered my question," I said.

The veterinarian working on my mangled hand never looked up, keeping his focus on his work, illuminated by a small headlamp he wore.

"We've been here since before it all began," Steven said, replying to what I'd asked a few minutes earlier.

"You saw it coming," I said.

"I've seen something coming for a long time," he said as he snipped bits of bluish skin away, leaving enough to create a flap that would seal the wound. "I bought this property ten years ago just before our son was born. Worked on it on weekends, over summers. Drove up from our home in Redding hundreds of times, hauling building supplies. Food. Water purifiers. Pumps."

"Do you have a radio?" I asked. "Anything to make contact?"

"Electronics invite detection," Steven answered. "I focused on the essentials that would let us stay alive undetected."

"I crammed all that in just before the blight exploded," I said. "I already had a place, sorta remote. That's where my survival journey began."

"Your daughter wasn't born then," Steven said, doing the math in his head.

"No. I hadn't met my wife yet. That happened in Bandon."

He began to suture the skin folds, closing the wound.

"This Bandon place," he said. "You're telling the truth? There's a cure for the blight?"

"There is," I told him. "We've been seeding and replanting as fast as we can. There are two settlements near us doing the same."

"Are you getting outside help?"

"Not anymore," I told him, taking a few minutes to fill him in on what we'd experienced, and who we'd been in contact with. "The chances are there's no longer any functioning government."

"Did we have a functioning government before all this?" he asked, flashing a smile as he finished stitching me up. "Any antibiotic allergies?"

"Do I answer with a woof?"

"I'll take that as a no," Steven said, then gave me an injection in my upper arm before bandaging the freshly closed wound. "It's gonna hurt for a while, and you'll need to keep it clean. As clean as possible."

"Will do," I said.

Steven put his tools and supplies back in their case and scooped the trash into a small sack which he tied and placed atop the mantle for later burning. Finished, he looked back to me.

"How long do you think until these people make a move on this cabin?"

I thought for a moment, listening to the steady rain pound outside.

"I don't know that I see his people pushing through this weather," I said. "They have numbers, but most aren't great physical specimens."

"Storms like this are usually over by dawn," Steven said, thinking for a moment. "I'll move the family to a deeper hide then."

"Good idea," I said, admiring the man and what he'd accomplished. "You keep your food and supplies away from where you lay your head. That's smart."

"It keeps us mobile," Steven explained. "Though we haven't really had to bug out from this place for, oh, must be three years now."

"That was your last contact?"

He nodded. I was certain he never expected any further contact with the outside world, likely believing that they might be the very last people alive. But they weren't.

"When this is over, we can send you seeds and plants," I told him.

"Fresh vegetables," Steven said, chuckling softly. "I don't even know that I remember—"

A sudden rush of sound from the kitchen drew his attention. And mine. It was Willow, dripping wet as he bolted into the room, muddy paws leaving thick tracks on the wood floor. Marcia and Neil hurried in behind her.

"He just flew through the dog door," Marcia said, worried.

Steven stood and faced his Doberman, the dog sitting now, looking up to him.

"Show me," he said.

Willow moved quickly to the front door. Steven blew out the candles and opened it. The dog walked out onto the covered porch, followed by the rest of us, Neil and I taking our AKs in hand. Near the east edge of the porch, with water pouring off the roof edge in front of him, Willow stared directly to the northeast.

"They're coming up the road," Steven said, looking to me. "Apparently they don't mind getting a little wet after all."

"He's pushing them," Neil said, looking to me. "Like riding a horse until it drops."

Steven looked back to his wife.

"Get our go bags and weapons," he instructed her. "Tell the kids we're moving now."

Twenty Four

We moved through the downpour, Neil and I bringing up the rear, Steven at the front, his family filling the space between us. In the dark it was impossible to miss puddles and trip over the dead roots of toppled trees, the littlest of our number, Penny, tumbling half a dozen times in the first twenty minutes after we'd fled the backwoods cabin.

"How far, Steven?" I asked.

"A quarter mile more," he said.

That was twenty minutes in these conditions. But, in less than one minute, we were stopped cold by a sharp explosion from behind.

From where we'd come.

Neil and I took positions to cover the family as Steven got his wife and children behind a pair of trees. In the distance, even through the pounding rain, we could all see the remnants of a fireball rolling into the wet darkness above, leaving a column of hot orange flames at its point of origin.

"They blew the cabin," Neil said.

"Mommy, our house," Penny said, her mother clutching her.

"We have other houses, baby," Marcia comforted her.

But I could see the woman's gaze, even in the weak light the night allowed. It was fixed upon me with pure terror brimming.

"Let's move," Steven said.

"Go," I said. "Neil and I will hang back to make sure no one follows."

Steven moved toward his wife and children and helped them up, taking his little girl in his arms so they could move more quickly. I focused on Marcia and gave her a nod.

"No one's getting to you," I said.

"Marcia..."

She hesitated for just a few seconds, staring at me, as if trying to decide if I was the kind of man who could deliver on the promise I'd just made. Before she came to any obvious conclusion her husband pulled her away.

"They won't know how to find us," she told him.

"That's probably better," Neil said, answering exactly as I would have.

In thirty seconds they were gone, disappearing to the west. Somewhere ahead of them Willow had been sent to scout. If there was trouble in that direction, he would warn them.

"What do you want to do?" I asked Neil.

He stayed focused on the dimming fire in the distance, the storm beginning to quench its initial fury.

"We have to lead them away from those children," he said.

"Agreed," I said. "North of the lake, then?"

"Right."

The family was moving to a hideout somewhere south of the lake, likely in dense woods. Our move would, if executed properly, keep Perkins far from them. To manage that, though, we would have to lure his fighters into skirmishes where we could take them on in smaller numbers.

"Let's move due north right now and set up an overwatch position," Neil suggested. "If they shift south, we can see it and move on their flank."

It was a solid tactical plan, but it would require one thing that was out of our control.

"This will only work if we can see them," I reminded my friend.

"They've got their bonfire," Neil said. "Perkins will want to check the rubble for our bodies. That won't be cool before sunrise."

He had a point. It was possible that Perkins believed he'd cornered us in the cabin and had ordered it demolished when no response came to his demands to surrender. The evidence of that success or failure lay in a pile of blazing timbers.

"Let's find a spot," I said.

I moved from behind the tree, ready to head north. Neil's sudden grip on my shirt stopped me.

"Just so we're in agreement," he began, "we're either ending Perkins right here on this mountain, or we die trying."

That wasn't at all how our mad dash to freedom had been envisioned back in Klamath Falls. Nor when we eliminated the scouting party in Tulelake. But here, on this mountain, that was precisely what it had turned into.

Twenty Five

The storm stopped before first light, just as Steven had said it would.

"We don't even know their last name," I said, soaked to the bone.

"They didn't offer it," Neil said. "You told them ours and they withheld theirs."

I didn't know why that just-realized fact puzzled me, but it did. It was just a minor curiosity in a world wiped of things such as anonymity. There was little reason to deny information about one's self to others. Nothing could be exploited from it. There was no identity theft.

There was subterfuge, though. Revelations about my friend had taught me that. The lie was more useful than silence, it turned out. For him, at least.

Until that was turned against him.

General Weatherly had put the screws to him once the truth of his duplicitous defection to the Unified Government had been revealed. Perkins, too, had seen opportunity in Neil Moore.

Me...all I cared about was that I had my friend back.

"It was probably Smith," Neil said. "Something obvious."

"I'll ask them once this is over," I said.

The sun began to rise in earnest, rays of daylight slicing through holes in the clouds. We were positioned beneath and behind a rocky outcropping on a slope above the northern shore of Medicine Lake, shivering and hungry.

The meal that Marcia had been in the process of preparing, cold as it was, had never been served, its ingredients shoved into her children's backpacks as we fled the cabin. Once more we were running on will, any strength to be summoned fueled by adrenalin.

The first burst of that came with the sound of engines. Multiple engines.

"I hear three," Neil said.

"Trucks," I added.

He nodded and we readied our position, resting the barrels of our AKs on shelves of small boulders we'd spent the dark hours arranging for just such a purpose. We had no more ammunition than when we'd begun our climb to Medicine Lake, nine spare magazines between us, a combination of what we'd left Klamath Falls with and those scavenged after the ambush at the warehouse complex. With three grenades added to the mix, we could put up a fight, but it would have to be on our terms.

"Which way are we going if this goes down?" Neil asked.

We'd considered two avenues of egress from our position once the fighting broke out, allowing us to shoot and move, keeping the attackers off balance and unsure of where we were. From our current spot we could shift to a higher vantage, or a lower one. Each had its combination of advantages and disadvantages.

"Let's go higher," I said.

"Okay."

Whoever came at us would have to fight their way up the slope, crossing uneven and open terrain.

"There they are," I said.

The trio of trucks we'd heard were easy enough to spot, as were the dozens of fighters on foot flanking the transports. It was almost certain that a dozen or more enemy were out of sight, held back in the woods, ready to provide supporting fire if that became necessary. And it would become necessary, we both knew.

"Fletch..."

"I see it."

The convoy was splitting up, with two trucks turning to follow the south shore of the lake, and one moving along the road closest to us. An equal ratio of fighters divided up with each, leaving the smallest force closing unknowingly in on our position while the other pushed in a direction we had hoped to prevent.

"They could be rolling right on top of that family in a few minutes," Neil said.

We didn't know the precise location of the hideout the family had moved to, but the two dozen fighters on foot fanning out into the woods that were nestled next to the lake were uncomfortably close to where they might be. That was a risk neither of us were willing to take.

"We hit this element when it gets below us," I said. "That will draw the others back to our side of the lake."

"They'll have to backtrack," Neil said, agreeing. "We'll have time to reposition."

If we could completely destroy the vehicle and the dozen armed foot soldiers attached to it, we would significantly improve our odds. With the advantage of elevation and surprise, not to mention the almost certain lack of battle hardening some of those below us would possess, I believed this was our best opportunity.

"You handle grenades if we need them," Neil said. "You have a better arm."

I set the trio of fragmentation grenades on a low rock between us. If it came to needing them, I would only need to pull the pin and roll one down the slope. The blast alone might drive anyone advancing back, forcing them to take cover.

"There's going to be a hell of a lot of lead flying," I reminded my friend.

"Ours first," Neil said.

"Damn straight," I agreed.

We kept our heads down and listened, the rumble of the single truck growing louder on the road a hundred and fifty feet below us. We waited. And waited.

"You ready?" I asked.

Neil nodded. The sound was directly below our position now. Our time to act had come.

Twenty Six

We both rose from behind the rock outcropping and took aim at the vehicle and those around it. In unison we began firing, squeezing single, aimed shots to conserve our ammunition. I concentrated on the cab of the truck with my first few rounds, punching holes in the roof above the unseen driver. The beefy vehicle lurched forward and swung to the left, careening off the road and rolling over on the rocky shoulder, tumbling violently until it splashed into the crystalline waters of the lake.

The foot soldiers who'd survived our first volley, eight in number, abandoned their wounded and dead comrades on the road, scrambling for cover. Across the lake, reacting to the sudden assault, one of the SAWs was opening up, its rounds falling wildly short across the wide body of water.

"They're pushed up against the slope," Neil said. "Out of sight."

The eight survivors, cowering now, were in good cover. That was about to change. I picked up one grenade and pulled the pin, releasing the handle and setting the fuse to sizzle. I lobbed it over the natural parapet before us and watched it bounce once, twice, then, before it could impact the asphalt road it detonated.

Screams rose as some of the shrapnel found its mark. More importantly, those who'd been in cover ran into the open. Two actually went to their knees and brought their weapons into the fight, one an AK and the other a pump shotgun, the latter ill suited to the battle now unfolding. I fired at the fighter wielding the AK, as did Neil, dropping the man with a combined four shots. We shifted our focus to the man with the shotgun, who turned out not to be a man, the woman's long red hair billowing in a sudden gust as she stood defiantly and fired at our position until her weapon ran out of ammunition. A single shot from my friend dispatched the woman, dropping her in the middle of the road.

The movement below us ceased, just muffled moans left to mark the results of the ambush we'd sprung.

"They're regrouping," I said.

Neil looked across the lake and saw what I did. The two other trucks were turning around, about half the fighters climbing aboard while the others began running to reach our side of the lake. The SAW had stopped its pointless waste of ammo, some discipline coming to the reaction.

"Bryce is over there," Neil said. "He's maneuvering them. Look."

My friend was right. The disciplined group running to confront us was dividing into sections, three groups of four, one moving into the tree line to conceal their movement. The former Air Force PJ was putting his experience to use.

And we had to be ready for that.

"Let's move," I said.

We gathered only our weapons and ammo. I pocketed the remaining two grenades and followed Neil as he began working his way up to the second position we'd scouted a hundred feet higher up the mountain, staying low to use the cover afforded by boulders and slabs of volcanic rock which covered the slope.

"You think we're lucky enough that Perkins was in that first truck?" Neil wondered, waiting through the silence that was my response. "Yeah, me neither."

In five minutes, as we were about to reach our second position, the incoming fire started up again, more accurate this time, chunks of rock splintering both above and below us. A quick look placed the source of the fire, and it wasn't from the element which had initially moved south.

"The reserves are moving," I said.

There were twenty of them by my rough count, pouring out of the woods along the road, closer than the elements which Bryce was presumably leading. They weren't as well ordered, but they weren't fodder, either, moving and covering as they bounded toward the trail which would allow them access to the positions we'd staked out.

Neil knelt behind a low, gnarled basalt boulder and squeezed off four rounds before ducking away from a volley of fire that was almost on the money. Twenty feet to his right, I surveyed the damage through a space between a pile of rocky deposits left by some old avalanche.

"One down," I reported.

"The math isn't going to work in our favor," he said.

With the limited amount of rounds we had, our weapons would run dry before the last of Perkins' fighters were upon us. Our shots had to count. Every last one of them.

"We pop up and each fire once," I said. "I'll take the front of the group, you take the rear. We'll meet in the middle."

Neil nodded. I readied my AK and looked to my friend. We needed no silent countdown. Just a look signaled when we were both ready, and we quickly rose above our stony shields, squeezing off a single shot each. Before I dropped back down amidst bullets whizzing past and ricocheting off the surrounding rocks I saw my target fall.

"One down," I said.

"I missed," Neil said, shooting me a frustrated glance.

"Get 'em on the next one," I said.

Once more we looked to each other, waiting for the right moment, both of us ready to rise once again. But neither of us did.

The sound of the aircraft buzzing directly overhead kept our heads down. It had come over the top of the slope we were pressed against, its approach hidden until the last second. It was the Cessna that I'd arrived on, in possession of Perkins' forces now, the craft circling back toward us after flying out over the lake.

"They called the bird in on us," Neil said.

"It's going to be their eye in the sky," I said.

Spotting us from the air and radioing our position and movements would turn the already formidable odds against us into something almost insurmountable. Yet we couldn't waste ammunition hoping for a lucky shot to bring the aircraft down, or at least drive it off.

"We could use Grace right about now," Neil said.

She'd taken down the attacking helicopter back in Montana with a single shot from a hunting rifle, her true aim eliminating the pilot. This was different, though.

"This target's a little faster," I said.

"I'd still put money on her," Neil said.

The Cessna was barreling down on us again, but we still had the advancing fighters below to deal with. And those led by Bryce not far behind.

"Another round on us?" Neil said.

I nodded. We readied ourselves and rose up, firing a single shot each, a pair of our enemy falling as the Cessna screamed overhead and the mountain around us exploded.

Twenty Seven

For an instant I didn't realize that the sound and the fury suddenly enveloping us wasn't simply from the rounds we'd fired. Then, in the next instant, with the concussive force of the blast knocking me twenty feet down the trail we'd climbed, that part of my brain which processed such things uttered a single internal word.

Bomb...

"Fletch!"

Neil had recovered from the explosion and was racing down the trail toward me, both my weapon and his in hand as he hunched low to avoid the increasing fire. He reached me and pulled me to a sitting position against the rocks, checking me over quickly.

"You're not hurt," he said. "You're okay. You're okay."

I looked to him, still stunned, though the shock was wearing off.

"He's coming around again, Fletch. We've gotta get off this slope."

My wits quickly returning, I looked around, understanding what my friend was saying. Up here, where we'd believed we held an advantage, we had unintentionally made ourselves the perfect target for an aerial attack. With no friendlies surrounding us, the Cessna could make pass after pass, dropping explosives upon us until one found its mark.

"We've gotta get down there and fight close," Neil said.

I looked to him and nodded. There was more than agreement in the gesture—there was acknowledgement. An acceptance of what that course of action meant.

We would be able to fight, but there would be no coming out the other side for us. The measure of success would not be our survival, but rather how many of Perkins' people we could take with us before we were killed.

This was the end.

I reached out and took my AK. Neil held out one of the two remaining grenades.

"I'm good with just this," I said, readying my AK.

Neil kept it and pulled the pin.

"We've gotta hoof it fast," he said. "You ready?"

I came to my feet, crouched low with my AK ready. Neil popped up and threw the grenade down toward the closing fighters and ran past me, taking the lead. I followed, both of us scrambling down the trail we'd just come up, rounds zipping past us as the grenade exploded below. I glanced quickly toward our enemies and saw them take cover only momentarily before moving again, weapons up, firing at us. I stopped for a second only and fired two shots, one person at the head of their advance crumpling to the ground.

"Covering!" Neil shouted. "Go!"

He'd dropped to a knee next to a smooth boulder and fired back at our pursuers as I dashed past him, leapfrogging ahead twenty yards.

Then the plane came back.

I looked up from just past our first position and saw three or four objects fall from the Cessna, each arcing ballistically toward us, one different than the others, smoke trailing from it.

Dynamite...

The slender cylinder of explosives hit the slope above us and bounced down toward the trail we were on, its fuse burning. Higher up the other objects detonated, shrapnel from each peppering the area we'd just left. They were grenades, I realized, but there was no time to say so aloud as Neil and I dove for cover.

The dynamite exploded on the slope above and between us, sending a rockfall cascading down over the trail. It was far enough and blocked by terrain that there was no concussive effect this time, but the obstacle it had created between my friend and me was formidable.

"Neil!"

"Go down, Fletch! I'll work my way around the back side!"

The trail we'd followed split into a second avenue of approach just before the obstacle on Neil's side. It was a harder path to egress, but there was no choice for my friend. Were he to try and scramble over the mini avalanche he would be fully exposed to fire from below. I hated the fact, but for the moment we would have to split up.

"I'll see you at the bottom!" I shouted.

I began to move again, rushing to reach the base of the trail before the advancing fighters could cut me off. Every fifty feet or so, with withering fire pouring in, I would pop up and fire a few shots, maybe a third of each volley finding their mark. By the time I reached the base of the trail I'd burned through two magazines and had only one spare to go with the full one in my AK.

Then, once more, I heard the plane coming in.

I was in the trees now that followed the shore to the west end of the lake, and the Cessna was high above to the east, setting up for another run. Bits of dead trees all around me splintered with dozens of impacts from bursts of automatic fire aimed at me. Moving from tree to tree, and rock to rock, I kept looking past the base of the trail to the deep gulley that ran down the reverse side of the slope. Neil should be coming out there. Should have come out from there already.

But he hadn't.

Steady fire from our enemy kept me from moving that way, and the sight of the Cessna now descending, its nose pointed directly at me, forced me to shift more to the west into a thinning stand of trees which provided little cover. In that moment I realized that whatever trouble Neil was in, whatever test he was facing, my situation was no better. I was about to be hit from the air and overrun on the ground.

I brought my AK up and squeezed off rounds between the trees at any movement I saw, a wall of muzzle flashes facing me less than a hundred yards away. And from the corner of my eye I could plainly see the Cessna closing in, almost diving, setting up for another bombing run.

Then, I saw something else. From the same corner of my eye. Another aircraft. *The* other aircraft. The grey Cessna 172 swooped in from the south, lining up alongside its white twin and slightly behind. I swore I saw bright pulses from the new arrival, but could they be what I thought they were?

Muzzle flashes?

What happened next made it very clear that I'd been correct. The Cessna that had been setting up for an attack on me wobbled suddenly, as if in the throes of some spasm, then it rolled over on its side and nosed down into the center of the lake at a steep angle, trailing a thin ribbon of smoke. The impact obliterated the small aircraft and sent a geyser of water briefly into the air, marking its watery grave.

It also gave me a brief reprieve, but one with seemingly deadly consequences.

The advancing fighters who'd been pushing toward me stopped and directed their fire into the air, zeroing in on the Grey aircraft that could not avoid the phalanx of rounds being sent its way. It, too, shuddered midair and banked sharply, swinging from west to east, dropping rapidly as billowing white smoke poured from its engine, which sputtered and died just as the plane came down hard along the south shore of Medicine Lake. The tail was sheared off, the back half of the aircraft ripping away as it slid to the right, one wing crumpling in a ball of fire as spilling fuel ignited.

The threat to me from the air was gone, but that on the ground was still there, and it was moving again in my direction. Worse, though, was the reality that this force stood between me and Neil. If we were going to go down, which we'd mentally prepared ourselves for, I'd rather that happen together, and I knew my friend felt the same way.

I fired and moved, once more shifting south, though any further movement in that direction would negate the entire purpose of our strategy—to keep Perkins and his followers away from the innocent family. The fighters adjusted their own advance, following me through woods that began to mimic the field of blowdown Neil and I had come across the previous day. That afforded me more opportunities for cover, but slowed me greatly. As I positioned myself behind a low pile of decaying logs I squeezed off a series of rounds, noting only one enemy falling. Worse still, my magazine ran out and I was forced to insert the last one I had.

Thirty rounds were all that stood between me and certain death.

boom...

The explosion was distant and muffled. Mixed in amongst the waves of automatic fire, both near and far, I could not be certain that it was a grenade detonating, but it did sound like that. Neil had the last grenade, and I wondered if I'd just heard him laying waste to those threatening him, or employing the device as a last resort to take out the enemy overrunning his position.

I wanted desperately to be at his side, and to have him by mine, but what I saw out in the woods made me realize that was never going to happen. The enemy was splitting into three elements, some more coordination occurring. If Neil was correct in his estimation of the man, it would be Bryce directing this part of the battle. It wasn't a simple flanking maneuver I was facing, it was two, combined with a frontal assault, a full forty fighters moving on me. Echoing my friend's assessment just from just minutes earlier, the math wasn't on my side.

Until it was.

I heard the fire before I saw anything, a volley of controlled bursts coming from behind and to my right. Across the field littered with dead trees I noticed the enemy ducking, and then the eruption of impacts on the decaying pines became apparent as incoming rounds tore into their ranks. I heard screams and saw Perkins' fighters drop, first in ones and twos, and then in whole lines as they began to run. I chanced a quick look behind, and that was when I saw what, and who, had forced their retreat.

Six men had emerged from the woods on the south side of the lake. Two moving to the burning Cessna to pull the pilot free as the others directed expert fire upon those who'd been ready to take me out. I could only make out the barest details of the unknown force which had appeared from nowhere, noting that there seemed to be no standard attire among them. No shared uniform. But they moved and operated as a cohesive unit.

Next, I heard single rifle shots emanating from beyond their position near the downed plane. A sniper was firing. Another look toward the enemy allowed me to see three drop, and then a fourth as the long rifleman found his mark again and again. As I watched this I began to realize that not only were Perkins' people on the run or dying, the slice of land they'd abandoned was exactly the route I needed to cross to reach where my friend should be.

I had to find him. I had to get to him.

Staying low I moved to my left and bounded from tree to tree, seeking cover as I ventured into the woods that, until a minute ago, had been swarming with enemy. The fire from the unknown unit continued behind me and seemed to be shifting east along the lake shore, though I could no longer see any of it. Return fire from Perkins' followers had slowed, and with every twenty yards I crossed the volume of resistance seemed to decrease.

When I saw the bodies I understood why.

The fire from the new arrivals had not just been coordinated—it had been hellishly accurate. Dozens of fighters, men and some women, lay close to each other, some piled upon others, only a few still breathing, though their last breaths would not be long in coming. I gathered five spare magazines from the bodies and disarmed those who had not yet passed, wanting no surprise fire from behind. It could be said that I should have dispatched them with *coup de grace* shots, but I did not. The basic humanity I still held dear, though, was not what prevented me from doing what was tactically warranted—I simply did not want to announce my presence with fire in the no man's land. That would have been far from wise. Instead I moved quickly but cautiously, checking my six until there was no more to scan for.

I had reached empty woods.

In many ways that was more unsettling. Even with the bursts of distant fire signaling that the fight was still on, the swath of grey terrain I moved through felt eerily empty. Even isolated. But it wasn't either, and I learned that first hand when the wooden butt of a swinging rifle glanced off my left shoulder and smashed against my face.

Twenty Eight

The impact stunned me, the instantaneous fog filling my head different than that which had come from the proximity to the blasts just moments ago. There I had been subjected to an almost smothering pressure, delivered anonymously, which ripped the breath from my lungs. Here, a person had struck me.

A woman.

"You son of a bitch," Sheryl Quincy said.

She stood over me, I saw as I regained some mental focus. The same return of awareness allowed me to realize that my rifle was no longer in my grip, but rather lying at an angle across my bent legs where I lay on the forest floor.

"You couldn't just sign on when the Unified Government came," she said, staring at me past the fat muzzle of a sawed-off pump shotgun, rage and tears in her eyes. "You had to be top dogs. You had to push everyone away."

With every word the weapon in her hands stabbed at me, as if she was threatening me with some medieval lance she wielded.

"And now...this."

She didn't point or gesture, leaving me to interpret what was fueling her burning hatred beyond what she'd felt toward me. Could it be the body count of her brethren, already in the dozens with the firefight continuing closer to the lake? Or was it something deeper?

"I would have been on top," she said, openly weeping now. "Up top with...with him."

What was she saying? That she'd expected to ride the wave of conquest alongside Earl Perkins and be his co-ruler? But ruler over what?

"This was never going to end the way you wanted it, Sheryl," I said.

Her face tightened at my statement, the reaction all too similar to how her man had shown his displeasure with any display of insolence. They were meant for each other, I thought.

"That may be," she said. "But I certainly know how you're going to end."

A slight pressure on the trigger would end my life. This I knew beyond a doubt. And she was about to make that the last reality I would know.

But before that came to pass, a series of things happened in quick succession. Almost too quick to process at the moment each occurred nearly simultaneously.

A black blur burst into view from her right, launching through the air like a shadowy rocket, impacting the woman who was about to kill me and knocking her into a tree as she pulled the trigger. The shotgun blast, knocked off aim by the unexpected strike on her, hit the ground to my right, sending a shower of dirt and splintered branches into the air. As the debris rained down over me I grabbed my AK and rolled, coming up to one knee next to a nearby pine as the first inkling of what had actually happened became clear.

Ripping. That was what I heard. The sound of flesh being torn and shredded. Along with this was mixed a sickening wet gurgling, and through that some feeble attempt at a scream. As the dust from the thankfully errant shotgun blast cleared, I saw the source of these terrible sounds.

Sheryl Quincy, traitor and wannabe consort of the newest dictator to rise in our blighted world, lay on the ground on her back, sawed-off shotgun a few feet away, her hands vainly clawing at the Doberman whose jaws were clamped onto the front of her neck.

Willow had come from nowhere, which was exactly what she'd been trained to do. This, though, was not in the repertoire she had learned. Or her master hadn't shared all that she'd been trained to do. Whatever the motivation which had driven the dog's actions, she was seeing her attack through to the end, whipping her head back and forth to cause more damage, blood pouring out of her clenched jaws and painting Sheryl Quincy's upper half a deep, dark red. The woman swatted at the dog once more, then her arms fell to her side, her body stilling, the rise of fall of her chest, which had been erratic, ceasing entirely.

She was dead.

Sensing her kill was complete, Willow released her hold on the target of her attack and backed away, turning her attention to me. It was not an aggressive stance she took. Her muzzle, dripping blood, was closed, no teeth bared in any threatening manner. She seemed, instead, to simply be looking me over, as if judging whether I was all right.

Then, a moment later, her survey of my condition done, she turned and bolted off, running south through the grey woods. Gone as quickly as she had come.

I could have ruminated on what had just happened, but there was no time. I had my own place to be, and that was wherever Neil was. I rose to me feet and began to move, more quickly now, the sounds of battle decreasing as I plunged back into the battlefield ahead. Or what had been the battlefield, the scattered bodies thicker the closer I came to the western edge of the lake.

Nearing the edge of the woods, with the slope of the mountain ahead where Neil and I had been separated, I slowed once again and hugged the tree line, a group of five men just ahead, one of them limping, their weapons up and aimed forward. They were from the unit which had appeared on the south side of the lake after the plane's hard landing on the shore, their mixed attire more visible now, a mix of jeans and BDU pants and camouflage shirts. Every last one of them, though, wore the familiar US military Kevlar helmet, with one distinguishing feature stenciled on the back—USMC.

Marines...

I didn't know how that was possible. But they, at the very least, were the enemy of my enemy. What that meant I wasn't sure, but I would soon find out.

"Friendly!" I shouted.

I had no choice but to announce myself, the unit directly between me and where I needed to be. In unison three of the Marines swung my way, the others maintaining their focus forward. My weapon was pointed at the ground, that, and my calling out to them, enough to forestall any attack.

One of the Marines took a few steps my way, his M-16 pointed right at my chest. Until it was not. He shifted his aim off of me and looked me straight in the eye.

"He's a friendly," the Marine said.

His ragtag uniform still bore a name stitched onto the breast—Mason.

Mason...

Mason?

The stuttering thought, and its accompanying recognition, stunned me for a moment. Until I heard another Marine call out a crushing report.

"Wounded friendly up here!"

I looked, as did Mason, both of us fixing our attention to a spot where the slope curved around to the trail on the backside. The very spot where I'd expected to Neil to appear.

And there he was, lying against a stump, waving one bloodied hand weakly before him to signal 'cease fire', that motion enough to let the approaching unit believe that he was not a threat.

"Neil!"

I bolted from the edge of the tree line, running past more bodies as Mason and the other Marines followed, moving cautiously. I was not, racing at full bore, leaping over bodies, one I recognized as Bryce, his right leg blown nearly off. That could have been what I'd heard—the grenade Neil had kept with him. He might have used it against the former Air Force PJ during a frantic confrontation.

As it turned out, I was only partly right.

I dropped my AK and knelt next to my friend, checking him over.

"You missed all the fun," Neil said, a catch in his breath that worried me.

As did the blood spurting from three holes in the front of his shirt.

"I got the son of a bitch," my friend said, his head tipping to the left.

I tracked his gesture quickly and saw a familiar face.

Earl Perkins lay on his side, a knife stuck in the side of his neck, his huge revolver grasped in his dead hand.

"He and Bryce," Neil half gasped. "Not quick enough to take me down. Not before...before..."

He couldn't finish the statement. I slid close and eased my friend so that he lay against me, looking up to the Marines as they reached our position. Two continued past, checking for any lingering threats. Mason and another Marine, a sergeant with the name Pompana penned in black marker upon his helmet cover, helped their limping younger comrade to a rock that faced us.

"Sit here, Buller," Mason said.

The wounded private took a seat and winced as his leader pressed hard against the spot where blood was trickling from the back of his leg.

"Looks like the cavalry actually came," Neil joked, his swimming gaze finding me next. "This is a tough one, Fletch."

I looked to Mason, the impossibly familiar young officer. Then again, this had been a journey of impossibilities, including the fact that I was with my friend again.

For now.

"You have a medic?" I asked.

"Corpsman, Fletch," Neil corrected me, lifting one of his hands from where it lay against my stomach to eye the thick smear of blood upon it. "They're Marines. They drag Navy types with them to bandage their boo boos."

It was a gentle ribbing, but neither Mason or I saw any humor in the moment.

"Gunny, go get Doc Lockton," Mason said. "Make it quick."

"Aye, sir," the gunnery sergeant acknowledged.

He sprinted off as the other two Marines, both lance corporals as indicated by the crossed rifles beneath their single chevron, returned from their quick check of the area.

"It's clear, lieutenant," one of them reported.

"Kiplinger, set up an OP fifty yards into the woods," Mason directed, turning his attention to the other enlisted man. "Stans, get up that slope and overwatch our position here."

I was hearing this and all that was happening around us, but my focus was on my friend, who I was holding as he was dying.

Twenty Nine

"They're getting help," I told Neil.

Mason was tending to his lightly wounded Marine while Gunny Pompana was running in full gear along the shore toward the downed plane, where their corpsman, Doc Lockton, was presumably tending to the pilot they'd pulled from the wreckage. In a few minutes that man of medicine would be here, summoned to help my friend. To save my friend.

I feared, though, that was not to be.

"I did kill him, right?" Neil asked me, a few bloody bubbles appearing at the corner of his mouth.

"You got him," I confirmed.

Neil smiled, the trickle of aspirated blood spreading across his lips, leaving the impression of a garish gash upon his face. Perkins' demise pleased him, it was plain to see. Even through the pain and realization of his condition, he found satisfaction in knowing that the despot had fallen.

"You should have seen the look on his face when he saw my knife," he said.

"Willow took out Sheryl Quincy," I shared.

My friend chuckled weakly.

"Taken out by a dog," he said. "I'd say that's a fitting...a fitting..."

His words ended as a wave of pain rolled through him. Every muscle seemed to tighten as he curled into a ball, his head pressed against my chest

"It's gonna be okay," I told him.

His tensed body relaxed after a moment and he looked up at me.

"You're wondering," my friend said, still more bloody spittle bubbling at the corner of his mouth.

"Stop talking," I told him, looking down the shore toward the lake, searching for some sign of the corpsman. "I need help here!"

Mason looked over to me while he held pressure on Private Buller's superficial leg wound. A round had grazed the back of the young Marine's thigh, deep enough to open a collection of blood vessels, but he was alert and still held his weapon, ready to fight.

"The doc will be here," Mason assured me.

There was no treatment I could give my friend, though. No tourniquet to apply which would stop the hemorrhaging within his body. He'd taken three rounds just below center mass. Rifle rounds. At least one had exited I could tell by the warm wetness pumping from his back where it rested against my leg. They must have come from Bryce, I imagined, both he and Perkins confronting Neil before he bested them both. Sheryl Quincy had seen it all, I assumed, her man's death enraging her and causing her to seek me out. Why she hadn't dispatched Neil I didn't know. Perhaps he'd seemed gone already.

Or perhaps she wanted the full measure of her vengeance to be delivered upon me.

"It's okay to wonder," Neil said, his voice drifting down toward a whisper. "You've done this before. You want to be sure."

"Neil, just, hang on," I said, gripping his hand tight while cradling his head. "Where is the Doc?!"

"Johnny Tartek," my friend said, and I looked down at him. "Johnny Tartek."

I puzzled at what he'd said. It wasn't nonsense, but the name meant nothing. At least to me.

"What are you saying, Neil?"

For an instant a smile stretched across his lips, brightening his ashen face. Then, a few seconds later, the expression went slack. As did the rest of him. His body relaxed fully where it lay against me and his head tipped back ever so slightly in my arms, all tension gone from him.

Neil Moore was dead. For real this time.

I eased his body down to the ground and scooted back a foot or so, taking in the sight of him, lying there. Gone from my life again.

The Navy Corpsman, Chief Wally Lockton, arrived a few minutes later.

"He's gone, doc," Mason informed him.

Lockton did a quick check for vital signs, then looked to me.

"I'm sorry," he said.

I nodded acceptance of his condolences, then the Navy man found a discarded jacket and placed it over my friend's face.

"Doc," Mason said, getting his corpsman's attention. "Buller took a graze."

Lockton moved to the wounded Marine and began working on him. Mason shifted positions and sat on a rock a couple yards from me.

"Too much going on to chat," Mason said. "You're all right?"

I wasn't, but he was focusing on the physical aspect of injury.

"Just my hand from a few days ago," I said.

Mason nodded and shed his helmet before taking a seat on the ground facing me, his back against the stump of a snapped-off pine.

"I remember you," Mason said.

"I remember you, too," I said.

It had been more than two years, but his face, one of the first we'd seen when arriving in Colby, Kansas, stood out amongst the dearth of others to remember.

"Been a while," the young officer said, drawing a breath of the cool mountain air rolling in off the lake, the acrid scents of battle already dissipating.

"There's a family out there," I said. "South of the lake somewhere in hiding. Their dog...saved me."

"War dog in our midst, eh?" Mason commented, attempting to inject some lightness in the exchange. "I'll send an element out to make contact."

"I'll go with them," I said. "They won't recognize your men."

"Fair enough," Mason agreed.

I looked to the spot a few feet away where Neil lay under the jacket Doc Lockton had placed over his body, my gaze searching futilely for some sign of movement. Of breathing. Some indication that, yet again, my friend had cheated death.

Johnny Tartek...

His words didn't trouble me. They confused me. Why some random name whose meaning only he knew had been the final words he offered made no sense to me? Then again, the presence of the man sitting next to me didn't either.

"Can I ask how the hell you ended up here?"

Mason snickered lightly. He was tired, but not beaten. The youthfulness I remembered from his already toughened face back in Kansas had been replaced by twenty years of hard living crammed into only a few.

"We're on our way to Bandon," he said.

My puzzled silence opened the door for a more complete explanation.

"Major James and the Osprey he flew you back in never returned," the lieutenant said.

"I know," I told him.

"How do you know?"

I shared the events surrounding our return aboard the Osprey, and its conscription into our defense of Bandon against the advancing Unified Government forces. When I came to the part about the aircraft being downed during the battle at the Rogue River, Mason quieted. Captain Hogan and Lieutenant Grendel had died with their Marine commander that day, the actions of all three certainly saving not only my life, but the town of Bandon as well.

"I had no idea," Mason said. "Our satellite radio died right after you left. We couldn't transmit or receive. And our shorter range units failed one by one over the next few months. We had one radio left that could receive only, and that was in our aircraft. That's how we zeroed in on you. Your enemies didn't practice any sort of radio discipline. They were broadcasting their locations, and what they were seeing. They mentioned Bandon several times in exchanges. That's what got us interested."

"I'm glad you got interested," I said. "So you ended up leaving Kansas."

"Several of my guys heard you all talk about your town when you came to Colby," Mason explained. "After Major James didn't return, we had no contact. Zero. From anyone. Not HQ, not anywhere. We were totally on our own."

"And you were in command," I said.

"Yes," he confirmed. "A lowly louie as maybe the senior ranking Marine left on planet earth."

"You made the decision to leave."

"I had to," Mason said. "We had dwindling supplies and no resupply in sight. After six months the writing was on the wall."

I processed what he had said, some of the mental math tripping me up, along with the logistics.

"That makes it about an eighteen-month trip," I said. "Did you hoof it or have vehicles? Did you hop the plane ahead to scout your route?"

Mason smiled a knowing smile.

"No, we left our ride about fifteen miles south of here on a stretch of railroad track," he said.

His explanation didn't register for a moment. And then it did.

"Heckerford?"

The lieutenant nodded, that knowing smile now registering the same disbelief mine was.

"Ivan Heckerford," he said. "Craziest train engineer this side of anywhere."

The oddball train operator had picked us up after the downing of Air Force One and had transported us to the Marine contingent at Colby, Kansas. On the brief trip he'd regaled us with his unique manner of...everything.

"You made it all the way here," I said. "On a train. That's..."

"Incredible," Mason said. "I know. We've got a flatbed and crane with rails and supplies to repair track. Another flatbed where we'd transport the plane after breaking it down. We started with three fuel tankers and just shed the second one past the Nevada border. And all the creature comforts of a few boxcars for food and tired Marines. And my Navy doc."

I took that all in. All that was left of the 2nd Marine Expeditionary Force was this young officer and his eight men. The civilian, Heckerford, had hauled them and their supplies halfway across the country to reach the place I'd sought out when it was cryptically known as Eagle One. The fact that the town had decided to spread itself out into ten enclaves was not something I needed to share. Not right then. Because Lt. Mason, his men, and even Heckerford, weren't actually seeking a place.

They were seeking a future.

"Heckerford says we can move a bit south from here and then cut west to link up with a main line heading north," Lt. Mason shared. "We'll probably have to fix track and bridges along the way, but he thinks we can be within fifty miles of Bandon in a week or so."

"They probably think I'm dead by now," I said.

To that, the Marine officer shook his head.

"Not until they see your body, they won't," he said. "Considering how they jawed with my guys back in Colby, I'd say your people are a lot like my Marines. The missing are still fighting for their country, and for the Corps, until we find them doing that or with a cold steel bayonet in their dead hands and the enemy's blood dripping from it."

It wasn't quite the talk a recruiter would give a prospective Marine, but it was certainly persuasive. It was also right.

"They'll be looking," I said, accepting his observation.

"They'll have a big ass moving train to see," Mason said. "We can put a message on top for them."

I nodded. Off to my right, Gunny Pompana was returning, following the shore with a trio of other Marines, one supported between the others, his left leg heavily bandaged. Mason took a moment to make introductions. Sergeant Pedro Esteves and Private Evan O'Halloran were the ones who'd assisted Private Ian White to our position. He'd been piloting the aircraft and had taken a round through the thigh after it had penetrated the thin metal fuselage.

"Doc, how's Private White?" Mason asked.

The corpsman had obviously bandaged the Marine up after he was pulled from the burning plane and before he was summoned to our position.

"Patched up," Lockton reported. "I wish I was a cutter. There are some fragments deep in there."

"We have a doctor," I told them. "Former Navy. He can help him."

"Former Navy's all right by me," Lockton said.

I looked to Private White, M-16 still in his grip.

"Flying and shooting?" I asked.

The young Marine smiled and pointed his rifle off to the side, holding it one handed.

"Just stuck it out the passenger window and *br-rrr-rrr-rr*," White said, smiling and wincing simultaneously as Lockton adjusted his bandage.

"Fletch," Mason said, leaning a bit toward me. "It is Fletch, right?"

I nodded. He glanced toward Neil's body.

"I'm going to have my guys police up the enemy bodies and just lay them out in the woods," he explained. "But we have a fifteen-mile hike out of here and at least a week on a train. No refrigeration. No way to..."

He didn't need to explain any further.

"We'll bury him here," I said.

"Was he former military?" Gunny Pompana asked.

"CIA," I told them.

Mason nodded, thinking.

"We'll do it right," he said.

Thirty

While Mason set a detail to prepare a grave for Neil, I accompanied Gunny Pompana, Lance Corporal Stans, and Private O'Halloran on a search through the southern woods for the family. After an hour searching for signs of them, as well as tracks left by Willow, it was if they'd disappeared into the ether.

"They don't seem to want to be found," Pompana said.

A half mile south of the lake we stopped and I looked out through the stands of dead trees, scanning the emptiness.

"If you're out there Steven and Marcia, it's all right!" I shouted. "I'm with some Marines! The enemy is finished!"

We listened. Then listened some more. But there was nothing to hear.

"They might have been overrun," Stans suggested.

Pompana shot him a look, some silent caution against defeatist conjecture.

"We're going back to the town I told you about! You can come with us! We're fully supplied!" I waited for a moment, almost praying for a response. "It's safe! I promise you!"

We spent another hour searching, even circling back toward the rubbled cabin, but found no sign of Steven, or Marcia, or Timothy, or Penny. Or Willow.

"I think maybe you're right, Gunny," I said. "They just want to stay."

The family had helped Neil and me. Their dog had saved me. But there was nothing more I could do for them.

"Okay," I said. "We tried."

* * *

Two hours later, as the afternoon crept toward evening, I stood with the Marines and their Navy corpsman on a plateau just above the lake. A pile of dirt sat next to a rectangular hole dug and cut through the rocky volcanic soil, my friend resting four feet down, a Marine poncho covering him. I'd spent ten minutes carving his name and the particulars of his life into a section of old plank scavenged from the sides of one of the abandoned flatbed trucks smoldering along the road. The marker would in no way tell the full measure of who Neil Moore was, or who he was to me.

Mason said a few words, but I declined to do so. I'd said my misplaced goodbyes to him once before, when he was actually still alive. I didn't need to do so again.

The simple service complete, Private O'Halloran and Lance Corporal Kiplinger began shoveling dirt into the hole. In five minutes they had my friend covered, the earth above him compacted.

"You all right?" Mason asked me.

The others filtered away, heading down the trail from the plateau. Their gear was stowed in the woods a mile from the lake, and another fourteen from that point was where our ride was waiting. It was time to get moving, but the lieutenant sensed I was not yet ready.

"No," I said. "I'm not."

He quieted for a moment. I thought he was waiting for me to speak, but, in reality, he was crafting a response too wise for someone his age.

"I've never lost a man," Mason told me. "Not one. Had a couple go AWOL from Colby before we set out, but I left that hellhole with seven Marines and my Navy guy, and they're all still breathing cussing killers who I'd lay my life down for. You know what else, though?"

"What?"

"Every single one of us knows death," he said. "Death we feel every day. The death of everyone we knew. Our families, our friends. We exist in a world of ghosts, Fletch. My guys still wake up from nightmares drenched in sweat because their mothers, or their children, are crying out to them from some dark place. They force those moments down, but I see it. I see it in their eyes in quiet moments when they can't help but think, and remember. I even think a couple of my guys probably consider your friend down there to be the lucky one. That's a hard motivation to counter, but I have to."

He shook his head, as if trying to process it all. Everything. From the blight's arrival until now.

"Nothing in this world makes sense, Fletch, except your next breath. And the next one. And the next one. If I get my guys to Bandon and they're still taking that next breath, my mission will be a success. I'm not sure the ghosts at the Pentagon would agree, but, honestly, I don't give a damn."

What he'd said didn't just apply to the fighting men under him. Nor just to me. That simple ethos, taking the next breath, was what had kept Neil Moore alive through the horrors he suffered. He had no more breaths to take, but enough of us did that every sacrifice mattered. Every drop of blood shed was an ocean too much, but still it had been shed for a purpose.

"The next breath," I said.

"And the next one," Mason added.

It was time to go home, and to bring the brave men who'd come to our rescue to that place, so they could take their next breaths in peace.

Thirty One

We left my friend's grave and Medicine Lake at dusk and hiked south, leaving the mountain behind as night settled upon the Northern California landscape. By midnight we were back in the flatlands of once fertile farms fields. Near three in the morning, moving in a tactical column, with his fellow Marines having taken turns carrying Private White piggyback style throughout the trek, a long shadow began to resolve along a low berm in the distance.

We'd reached our ride home.

"I'll's be a son of a banshee," Heckerford said as he climbed down from the cab of his armored locomotive, recognizing me in a wash of dim light from a lantern he'd lit upon our arrival. "You's one of those folks from that town we's makin' our way to."

"I am, Mr. Heckerford," I said.

"Let's keep lights to a minimum," Mason directed. "Gunny, put a watch up and see that everybody gets some rack time. We're moving out at dawn."

"Aye, sir," Gunny Pompana acknowledged and set about carrying out the orders.

Heckerford shook my hand, eyeing me sideways for a moment.

"I's knows your name, but I don't remembers it," he said, grinning at me through the bushy hole in his grey beard.

"Just call me Fletch," I said.

"Eric Fletcher!" Heckerford shouted, slapping his thigh with force as he recalled fully his first meeting with me. "You's was with some other folks back between Salina and Colby. Is they's okay?"

I nodded. Schiavo, Martin, Genesee, and Carter Laws were all still alive and doing well.

Alive...

That was a privilege in this world, and it was not always afforded in perpetuity.

"The lieutenant said the enemy was talking abouts two of you's they was chasin'."

Mason, standing close enough to catch this part of the conversation, gave an upward nod to Heckerford.

"Not right now, Ivan," the Marine officer said.

Heckerford looked to Mason, then back to me, his expression going slack, the smile mostly hidden behind the mass of hair on his face.

"I's sorry," Heckerford said to me, sincere regret in his eyes. "I's didn't know."

"It's all right," I told the man.

"Ivan," Mason said.

"Yes, lieutenant?"

"The plane's gone," Mason explained. "If you want we can ditch that flat car."

The engineer thought for a moment, then nodded.

"First siding we's come by I'll's back in and rejigger what we's pulling," Heckerford said, waving the lantern he held toward the back of the train. "I'm gonna go box the tie down chains."

Mason approved with a nod, and Heckerford flashed me a more subdued smile before making his way toward the rear of the train.

"We've got MREs if you're hungry," Mason said. "Half a boxcar full of those nasty things."

"Yeah," I said, allowing a small chuckle. "I'm just about hungry enough to eat a couple."

Mason led me toward the boxcar. Just ahead of it was the flat car which had transported the scout plane. Discarding it would require uncoupling those behind it and pushing it off into a siding, as Heckerford described.

"It's fairly amazing that you were able to haul all this from Kansas," I said.

"Ivan doesn't understand the word impossible," Mason said. "If we came to a bad section of track, a stretch that was washed out, he'd show us how to lay new rails. We came to this one bridge in New Mexico that had to be reinforced, so we did that, but he said it still wouldn't support the entire train. What did good old Ivan do? Went across with the engine and had us unspool a hundred yards of steel cable so he could tow the rest of the cars across one by one."

"Only the weight of a single car on the bridge at a time," I said.

"He may be simple," Mason said. "But he's not dumb."

We reached the box car and the lieutenant retrieved a pair of MRE pouches for me.

"Thanks," I said.

He studied me for a moment in the near darkness. Behind him, Lance Corporal Stans was climbing the exterior ladder to the top of the box car, rifle slung and binoculars around his neck. He would be on first watch, I could see, and he immediately began scanning the surrounding terrain as he stood atop the train car.

"With Private White down, I'm going to need to count on your help," Mason said. "I know you're still hurting, but..."

"I'm going to do whatever it takes to get us to Bandon," I assured him.

"Glad to hear it, Fletch," Mason said, turning to leave me before returning for one last thing. "And I'm Nathaniel, by the way."

"It's good to know you, Nathaniel," I said.

The lieutenant left me. I took a few steps away from the train and sat down on the low side of the berm that supported the rails upon which it rode. Behind me the fighting men were quieting, settling in for an abbreviated night of shuteye. I suspected that I would eat, and then I would sleep. I would likely even dream. If I did, I hoped it would be of my friend, as he was in our youth, when we were young and dumb and invincible. Before life became real, and long before the world was torn apart. I just wanted to forget the here and the now and drift off into memories of times that were good. If only for one short night.

Reality could have me back tomorrow.

Thirty Two

We worked our way south, Heckerford's diesel locomotive hauling the mishmash of train cars along the rails at painfully slow speeds.

"We runs a bad rail at ten miles an hour we gonna be fine," he'd explained to me. "We runs it at fifteen we gonna be walkin' the rest of the way."

By 'the rest of the way', he meant to Bandon.

"Sure could be usin' that plane nows," he said.

The scout plane they'd carried with them on a flatbed where half of the Marine contingent now sunned themselves had been tasked with seeking out viable rail routes before it became engaged in tracking Perkins' large force. Without it, the feisty engineer was forced to rely upon old rail maps to plot a viable path to follow, using his knowledge of the rails to decide which routes were likely impassable due to years of neglect and weather.

"Better out west heres," he commented. "Ups in New England, WHEW, we'd be findin' ten miles of bad track for every good one. The rails don't likes goin' from ice to hot and back and forth."

I smiled at the man. Riding in the cab with him, the armored window covers folded down, was an oddly pleasing experience. Most of the next six days I spent with him scanning the tracks ahead for bad spots.

On the seventh day we heard the plane.

* * *

We had just emerged from a series of short tunnels and were rolling slowly along a stretch of track near Bailey Cove on Shasta Lake, Heckerford's plan to stop soon to refuel, a process that involved the Marines dragging hoses from the last tanker car being dragged along and hand cranking a pump until the locomotive's tanks were full. That, though, was going to have to wait.

"I hear it," Mason said as he hurried into the cab.

I'd been walking along the engine's exterior side walkway, passing Sgt. Estevez when the distinctive sound pierced the thrumming drone of the big diesel powerplants just feet from us. The sergeant had charged back to alert his commander as I hurried to the cab.

"Shoulds we stop, lieutenant?" Heckerford asked.

Mason looked to me.

"I can't think of anyone else who'd have a plane flying low," I told him. "We're only two-hundred miles from Bandon."

His concern, I knew, was the unknown. A stopped train was a sitting duck. A moving train was not, and could creep into another tunnel for cover.

But a train under cover could not be spotted, and, at the end of the day, with the likelihood that we were hearing a search plane from Bandon, we wanted to be seen.

"Bring it to a stop," Mason ordered.

He and I left the cab and crossed two cars behind the locomotive, passing his Marines and Doc Lockton.

"Is it a friendly, sir?" Private Buller asked, the bandage gone from his graze wound, just a reddish scar showing as he stood in shorts on the flat car.

"We're hoping," Mason said.

He reached the box car just as the train stopped and climbed the ladder to its roof. I followed, standing with him on the rusty surface which had largely been covered by white lines, crudely brushed on using grease from buckets used to lubricate the train's axles.

"You see it?" Mason asked.

I shook my head. In the mountainous terrain surrounding the meandering shore of Shasta Lake, sounds could be reflected and heard miles from their source. The aircraft could be on the far side of the bay we'd stopped along and it would never see us.

Or we it.

"There!"

The report came from the flat car just forward of the box car we stood upon. Private White, sitting on a storage box with his wounded leg propped on another, was pointing almost due north, to a spot near a ridgeline.

"I see it," I said, pointing as well.

Mason nodded. Down on the flat car, Heckerford had joined his passengers, most of whom were eagerly watching the slender white plane in the distance while holding their weapons at the ready—just in case.

"They're turning," I said.

The aircraft was banking sharply right in a deliberate manner until it was pointed directly at us.

"Gunny," Mason said, holding out a hand.

Below, Gunny Pompana, whose first name I'd learned was Zeke, tossed a pair of binoculars up to his commander. He brought them to his eyes and zeroed in on the approaching craft.

"It's a Cessna," he said. "A Two Oh Six."

I wasn't an expert on aircraft, but in my gut I knew I was looking at one of the planes Chris Beekman had salvaged from Ward Field after Dave Arndt and I had set out to scout as far as Klamath falls. And, also in said gut, I knew that the man himself would be piloting it.

"It's going to be upside down from the direction he's coming," Mason said, still focused in on the aircraft.

I glanced at the large block lettering on the roof near our feet, blazing white against rusty yellow, and smiled.

"If he can't figure out what *nodnaB* means, I don't want to be rescued by him," I said.

Less than a minute late the 206 buzzed right over our heads, then circled back and passed three more times, tipping its wings each time as we all waved madly at it. Then, for a few minutes, it orbited out over the lake before approaching again, slowing appreciably as it sailed above, something falling from the passenger side and landing fifty yards ahead on the track.

"Kiplinger," Gunny Pompana said.

Lance Corporal Dennis Kiplinger hopped down and raced to where the object lay, retrieving it and bringing it up to Lt. Mason as the aircraft resumed orbiting just over the bay.

"It has to be a message," I said.

"It is," Mason confirmed, unwrapping a slip of paper from a light stick it was tied to. "Fletch, is that you? If so, give a crossed arms on our next pass. If you need a radio, have man next to you give crossed arms. If radio required, will return tomorrow and drop one. Remain on same track if possible once you are moving. Beekman says nowhere safe to land. Martin."

Martin...

I looked to the aircraft and smiled. The man who'd led Bandon through its most trying times was riding shotgun with Beekman, serving as observer. As the 206 turned back toward us, both Mason and I held up crossed arms. It passed over once more, tipping its wings to acknowledge our reply, then gained altitude and headed north over the mountains.

Mason looked to me, smiling, then faced his men and Heckerford from his perch atop the box car.

"Bandon will be waiting for us," he said.

A cheer erupted, hugs being shared and backs being slapped. It was a moment of joy, but within it was a reality I now had to face—returning to Bandon meant sharing what had happened. And with whom.

"Nathaniel," I said, and Mason turned toward me. "I have to ask a favor."

"If I can make it happen, I will," he said.

"I believe you can," I told him.

When I was done he agreed, then moved among his men, speaking to each individually, finishing with the man driving us toward Bandon. When he was done he looked to me from the flat car and gave me a thumbs up.

As simple as the request turned out to be, a sense of relief came over me. Our arrival in Bandon would be an event. My return would carry with it a combination of difficulties and responsibilities. One responsibility in particular. It was that which I was hoping to manage with Mason's help.

All that remained was for me to do what had to be done.

Thirty Three

The next day, ten miles north of where we'd been spotted by the aircraft from Bandon, it came again as we worked to repair a fifty-foot length of rails knocked askew by an old landslide. Work stopped as the same Cessna 206 circled, then slowed and flew low, dropping another object, this one slowed by a small parachute affixed to it. A few minutes later, after unwrapping the protective cushioning applied to the contents, we had a working radio.

"You know them," Mason said, passing the handheld unit to me.

I turned the unit on and entered the frequency an attached note had specified.

"Martin, do you copy?"

I released the mic key and listened, waiting. The voice that replied was both welcome, and a surprise.

"You're late for dinner," Elaine said.

My eyes filled with tears, and I laughed softly before keying the radio again.

"Did you keep some warm for me?"

We exchanged small talk for a moment as the aircraft carrying my wife circled above, then I relayed the information about Dave Arndt's fate. That terrible event covered, we moved on to the particulars of how we would manage to reach Bandon. She reported that Beekman had surveyed the tracks that lay ahead and we were good until Medford, Oregon. Trucks from Bandon would be waiting there for us. I told her of the injuries of Private White's that would have to be treated upon our arrival in town, and, with Mason making a gesture to my own hand, I shared my own misfortune. She took the news well, but informed me I would be paying for any replacement wedding band. I said that was fair, as long as she sprung for a replacement finger.

It was difficult to end our conversation, but she and Beekman had to return, and we had to get the train moving again. I ended the exchange asking her to kiss our daughter for me.

"You could have talked longer," Mason said. "There are extra batteries in the drop they made."

"It's all right," I said. "We have our whole lives to talk when I get back."

What I didn't tell him was that, the longer we spoke, the harder it was to not tell her about Neil. That would have to wait, and I knew she would understand.

* * *

It took us three days to cover the hundred miles from our position north of Shasta Lake to Medford. Two trucks and a Humvee were waiting for us, with Martin, Schiavo, and Sergeant Hart, the medic bringing medication and fresh supplies so he and his Navy counterpart could begin prepping Private White's leg wound for eventual surgery.

"It's damn good to see you, Fletch," Martin said after the introductions were complete.

"You, too," I said, gesturing toward the now silent locomotive and the bearded man standing near it. "Go say hi before he loses it saying goodbye to his train."

Martin gave me a pat on the shoulder, leaving me with Schiavo. She had as much reason to greet Heckerford as her husband. Both had ridden with the man in Kansas. But, for some reason, she stayed with me, a concern about her.

"Perkins," she said, and I nodded. "Can't say I'm sad to hear he's gone."

"If anyone deserved it..."

"Was it you?" Schiavo asked. "Did you take him out?"

I hesitated, the line of her innocent question taking me by surprise. She seemed to notice the delay in my response, but I recovered as quickly as I could.

"No," I said, choosing a partly honest answer. "Someone else did."

She considered my answer for a moment, some wonder clearly bubbling beneath her reaction. But she didn't press me on the oddity she'd rightly sensed. She simply let it be.

"Well, whoever it was, they deserve a medal," she said.

I couldn't disagree with that, though a medal truly seemed an inadequate expression of gratitude for what Neil Moore had done. Maybe for this one action, and the price he'd paid, it was. But there was so much more that my friend had done, both for the town, and for me.

* * *

We left Medford and drove north, turning toward the coast and passing through Camas Valley and Remote before nearing the place which had seemed a beacon to the Marines from Kansas, and, much earlier, to me in Montana. Eagle One, Bandon—what the place was called didn't matter. What it had become did.

It was where survivors had fought against all odds, had confronted enemies and Mother Nature, only to grow stronger with each test. When it ultimately was split into scattered settlements, the physical town would remain, but the spirit that made it flourish would be planted in multiple locales. I knew that, when it was presented to them, the new arrivals from Kansas would embrace the change.

But that would come in time. As the vehicles turned into town and drove toward the hospital, I mentally prepared myself for what had to be done. For what I had to do.

I owed my friend Neil nothing less.

Part Five

The Return

Thirty Four

I'd sworn Heckerford and Lt. Mason and his troops to secrecy in regards to Neil. Not because I didn't want his story told, but because I had to be the one to tell it to those entitled to hear it.

"The stitching isn't bad," Clay Genesee said. "The corpsman did all right."

"It wasn't him," I said, my gaze cast slightly away from the wound he was examining. "There was a family we stumbled upon. The father was a veterinarian."

Genesee stopped his gentle probing and looked to me, puzzled.

"Why would the corpsman let a vet handle this?"

I looked him in the eye and shook my head.

"It was before the Marines showed up," I told him.

For a moment he just stared at me, trying to reconcile one particular aspect of what I'd said with what he understood about what I'd experienced. An understanding that was both right and wrong.

Very wrong.

"You said 'we'," Genesee said. "Dave was already dead, from what I was told."

He'd received a rudimentary briefing from Elaine after our radio contact north of Shasta Lake, with the particulars on incoming injuries requiring treatment. That information hadn't included what I'd withheld for very specific reasons.

"He was," I confirmed. "But someone else wasn't."

It took me ten minutes to share with him the story of Neil Moore, who'd died and come back and died again. He listened without saying a word, letting me talk until all that needed to be said was said.

All but one thing.

"Grace needs to hear this," he told me.

That had been what I'd planned to say in my very next breath, but he did so before I could, understanding the totality of the revelation instantly. I hadn't expected resistance from him, nor any burst of jealousy over the man who'd been loved by Grace before she loved him. What he understood intrinsically, though, was that that love had never ended. It had only changed.

"She deserves to know," Genesee said, taking a moment to rebandage my hand. "She deserves to know now."

* * *

Grace was tending to Private Ian White, cleaning his gunshot wound in preparation for surgery to remove some deeply embedded bullet fragments when her husband led me into the hospital's second treatment room.

"Did I hear correctly, Fletch?" Grace asked, smiling as she looked to me, fixing on my hand. "You lost your wedding ring?"

She'd reduced the wound to a friendly ribbing, something to keep my reunion with her and all who'd worried about me on the positive side. It was a simple quip to lighten the moment.

"Private White here got shot and didn't lose anything, so I don't know *what* your problem was," she added, drawing a smile from the young Marine she was tending to.

"Grace, Fletch needs to talk to you for a minute," Genesee said.

She nodded and kept working on Private White.

"Of course," she said. "Just let me debride the exit wound. Should be ten minutes."

Genesee stepped forward and gently slid the instrument tray aside as Grace looked up to him, puzzled.

"I'll finish up here," Genesee said, managing a smile that was flavored with both concern and reassurance. "Go have your talk now."

Her gaze lingered on her husband for a moment, then shifted to me, an odd wisp of wondering in it. She snapped her gloves off and dropped them in a bin by the door.

"Okay," she said. "Break room, Fletch?"

"That'll be fine," I told her.

* * *

Hot water sizzled in an electric kettle and a collection of teabags were arranged in a basket near a stack of mugs on the small room's counter. Neither of us wanted a drink. Not that kind of drink, at least.

"Fletch, have you seen Elaine yet?"

"Briefly when we pulled in," I told Grace as she stood next to a chair at the room's only table.

"Briefly," she parroted.

I nodded and sat down. She didn't.

"So you could be out of here right now with your wife and daughter and you choose to stick around so you can talk to me."

"Grace..."

"What is it, Fletch?" she pressed me, seeming to sense something more than simple conversation was about to take place. "What's going on?"

I'd thought about how to tell her on the journey home. I'd run through mental scripts of the exchange we would have. Every word required was one I'd practiced a dozen times in my head.

But all those words failed me.

"Neil is dead," I said.

Her gaze skewed at me, head cocking slightly.

"Right," she said. "He's been dead for years."

I shook my head and I saw the color drain from her face. She reached out and steadied herself on the back of the chair before her.

"That wasn't him," I said. "He was alive the whole time."

She smiled oddly at me and shook her head.

"Fletch, this is crazy. Why would you even..."

I stood now and walked to her, taking her free hand in my unbandaged one.

"He was alive, and I was with him," I told her.

"Was," she repeated, her breaths stuttering, little gasps of disbelief escaping.

Then, I told her. Within the first minute her knees went weak and I helped her into the chair and pulled mine close to face her. I'd spent ten minutes telling Genesee about all that had happened, but I sat with his wife for a half an hour, sharing every last detail. Answering every question she had. Reassuring her in every way I could.

"He knew about you and Clay," I said.

"You told him?"

I nodded and she squeezed my hand, the gesture one of comfort. She knew how difficult that had been for me.

"Even knowing that, he wanted nothing more than to get back here," I said. "He wanted to get back to you, to make sure you were all right."

She hadn't cried at all. Not yet. But when I told her about his concern, her eyes began to glisten.

"This is like a dream," she said. "It's like I'm floating."

"You're in a bit of shock," I said. "I was, too."

"But he was there for you," Grace said. "In front of you."

"I'm so sorry, Grace."

She'd been robbed twice of having some final moments with the man she'd loved. And lost. It wasn't fair. In many ways we'd become accustomed to the inequity of life in the blighted world, but some realities, such as this cruel one, still stung.

"What was the last thing he said?" she asked. "You were with him, you said. Did he say anything?"

"It didn't make any sense," I said. "Some name."

"What was the name?"

"Johnny Tartek," I said, recalling my friend's final words.

"The football player?" Grace asked, more curious than troubled.

Johnny Tartek...

It wasn't a name from nowhere, I suddenly realized. It was a name from our collective past.

"Neil said he took a hard hit from that kid in a high school football game," Grace said.

"That's right," I confirmed, more puzzled now than I'd been when the name was simply nonsense.

"Why would he use his last breaths to tell you that name?" Grace wondered.

Perhaps his dying mind was simply grasping back in time at memories, and that was what his madly firing synapses had dredged from deep within his fading consciousness. That was only conjecture, though, as likely as it was to be accurate. The ultimate truth lay somewhere beyond my ability to grasp.

"I don't know," I told Grace, offering the only truth I could right then. "I honestly don't know."

Thirty Five

What to do with those followers of Perkins who might remain in the area of Klamath Falls was dealt with in a meeting of the town council called the day after my return to Bandon. There was discussion about doing nothing, which centered around the hostility expressed toward our town, as well as the not insignificant fact that they had killed both Dave Arndt and Neil Moore.

"Let them rot," was Stu Parker's suggestion.

The Council's newest member, elected just weeks prior to our fateful scouting mission to Klamath Falls, was unequivocal in his harshness. He'd been a close friend of fellow Council member Dave Arndt, a man who would now be replaced on the governing body. That Stu was letting emotion color his judgment in the matter up for discussion did not surprise me.

That much of the remaining Council entertained the idea did.

"Fletch..."

Hannah Morse was the one who sought my input. I'd been asked to sit in on the meeting to provide any insight into the wayward colony of survivors from Yuma. I looked to her, then to Stu, then to Joel Matthews. Finally, I set my gaze on my wife, Mayor of Bandon and head of the now short-staffed Town Council. Two chairs were empty at the table, though—that which would have been occupied by Dave Arndt, and the seat next to my wife which would normally be filled by Schiavo as military advisor to the

Council. She had found herself assisting Lieutenants Paul Lorenzen and Nathaniel Mason begin discussions on what should be done with the Marines who had joined their Army counterparts in our now peaceful town.

Peaceful at the moment, I reminded myself. Had Perkins had his way, we would be in the fight for our lives in the coming weeks and months. That had not come to pass, though the people he'd prepared for just such a battle still existed in some numbers. What their intentions and motivations were at this very moment was impossible to know.

"There are women and children," I said, wanting to immediately throw a splash of cold water on Stu's almost brutal proposal. "They were followers. Their leader is dead. My guess is they don't know what to do."

"How many died in the fight with you and the Marines?" Hannah asked.

"From the time Neil and I escaped from Perkins, I'd estimate between seventy and eighty were killed," I answered.

"You said Perkins told you there were about four-hundred total in Klamath Falls?" Elaine asked, referencing the quick briefing I'd given the Council at the beginning of the meeting.

"Four hundred and five was his claim," I said. "From what I saw that looked to be accurate."

"That would leave over three hundred people out there who he taught to hate us," Stu commented. "And you think we should try to bring them into the fold? Send out the welcome wagon for them?"

"No one's said what we should do yet," Elaine cautioned the man. "Except you."

Stu eased back in his chair and absorbed the mild rebuke. As it was, my wife was just trying to get a handle on what the options were in dealing with the Yuma survivors before coming to a consensus. If that was even possible.

"They're not a fighting force," I said. "It's been two weeks since Perkins died. My best guess is that they are just trying to hang on."

"They haven't reached out," Joel said. "They have radios, from what you said. They monitored our communications."

"The repeater at Camas Valley should be able to hear any transmission," Hannah added, validating the point her fellow Council member was trying to make.

A point my wife made for all to hear.

"Why wouldn't they try to contact us if they wanted to put Perkins behind them?"

She asked the question directly to me. I suspected she also knew I would have no good answer, which I didn't. There were possible explanations, but possibilities weren't something she could abide by in her position. The fate and future of Bandon, and of its plans to diversify its population through new settlements, was in many ways in her hands.

"I don't know," I said.

Elaine nodded thoughtfully, accepting my honesty. She looked to her fellow Council members, waiting for any further input, but there was none. It was time to suggest a path forward. Time to initiate some action with regards to the remaining Yuma survivors.

"We can't do anything until we know if they're even still there," my wife said. "They could have scattered. They could be moving this way. We need information."

The other Council members, one by one, nodded. Even Stu Parker. When they'd offered their silent consent to whatever Elaine was thinking, she looked to me.

"Chris Beekman needs to take a look," she said. "I want him to have an observer who knows what to look for."

I hadn't expected that.

"Will you go, Eric?"

I wasn't Fletch to her. I never really had been. But I'd always been willing to do what was needed, when it was needed, even if not asked. Here, she was asking me to return to the place where I'd watched Dave Arndt die. Where I'd found my lifelong friend inexplicably alive, only to have him die in my arms once again.

"You don't have to make contact or land," she assured me.

"If we see anyone, we should be prepared to reach out," I told her.

"Leaflets," Hannah suggested.

Like some throwback to warfare in the previous century, we would be dropping messages to those who had expressed a desire to destroy us.

"Tell them to surrender?" Joel asked.

"Order them to," Stu said.

"How about we tell them to contact us by radio," Elaine said. "You'd be able to receive if you're overhead or nearby just like we did at the train."

I nodded. Then Stu leaned forward and planted his elbows on the conference table.

"Okay," he said. "Let's say you go there, and drop your little leaflets, and they call back on the radio. I can tell you first thing I want them to know—we want our dead back. Dave's body is still there, and if they've done anything to it I swear to—"

"Stu," Elaine said, interrupting him gently. "We'll make provisions to get our casualties returned. I promise you that."

She looked to me then. I'd noted her use of the plural in the statement. Besides Dave, Neil was still out there, far from Klamath Falls, in the grave we'd dug for him by Medicine Lake. If we were going to bring Dave home at some point, the same respect had to be afforded to my friend.

"We'll come up with some wording," Elaine said, looking to me. "You'll get Beekman on board?"

I nodded. Where the man had once seemed almost a reluctant member of our community, his experience supporting our mission to and from the threatening carrier off our shore had changed him somewhat. Not softened, but surfaced an openness about him. I though that, maybe for the first time, he felt useful, even integral to our success. And our survival.

"We'll wait for the report from the scouting mission before making any further plans," Elaine said. "Agreed?"

The other Council members each raised a hand as a formal affirmation of the decision. She nodded and looked to me.

"You're up," she said.

Once again, I was.

Thirty Six

Chris Beekman's overland scavenging mission to Ward Field in Northern California had yielded results better than he had imagined. Two Cessna 206 single engine aircraft had required only minimal work to make them airworthy after their disassembly and hauling back to Bandon.

One of them, though, he had special plans for.

"I'll have number two outfitted with pontoons in two weeks," Beekman told me as we flew over the mountains which filled the landscape between Bandon and Klamath Falls. "That will open up a whole new range of destinations. All we'll need is a long enough lake or a slow flowing river like the Coquille where it empties into the harbor."

We...

He was even talking like he was part of the town now, in addition to acting like it. He'd required no convincing at all to pilot this mission, and even suggested a safer approach to our destination, one where we would slowly circle the city in decreasing intervals. That would give me a chance to observe with caution, alerting him to any threat while it was still in the distance.

Any danger would initiate our retreat from the airspace over Klamath falls. The M4, muzzle down between my knees, was only for use in the worst-case scenario—that we should have to set down. That wasn't going to happen, I told myself. And I tried to make myself believe it.

"We're getting close," Beekman said.

He quieted and looked out the left window, staring briefly at the woods surrounding the town, a splash of false green still visible even after several storms over the past weeks.

"Dave was a good student," Beekman said. "A good pilot. A good friend."

He looked to me. I nodded but added no more. He was down there, we assumed. Still lying where he'd fallen. I doubted that Perkins would have had his people bother with a burial. And, as Elaine had assured Stu Parker at the Council meeting, we wouldn't leave him there. This trip, though, was not meant to bring him home. The most we could do was offer our respect as we passed over.

"I'll start a two-mile loop," Beekman said as he banked to the left, setting us up to circle Klamath Falls in a clockwise orbit. "You tell me when it's clear to close in a bit."

"Got it," I said.

I lifted the binoculars I'd brought and began scanning out the passenger side window beneath the right-side wing. It was easy enough to zero in on specific landmarks from memory, the bank building in which Neil and I had been held in particular. But I tried to focus on areas of the city closest to our flight path, specifically trying to spot any sentries which would alert the remaining population to our presence.

"No lookouts that I can see," I said.

"If you could they wouldn't be very good lookouts," Beekman reminded me.

We completed one full orbit of the city, then Beekman took us closer in by a quarter mile, the center of the city more visible now, streets and intersections looking much like I'd remembered them from my brief exposure.

Except for one thing. One horrific, undeniable thing.

"I see bodies," I told Beekman.

He kept his attention on flying, but shot a quick glance my way.

"How many?"

I lowered the binoculars and looked to him.

"A lot," I said.

Ten minutes later, after working our way closer to the apparent carnage I'd spotted, Beekman took us down low, just a few hundred feet off the ground, the Cessna cruising parallel to a main thoroughfare so that I could plainly view the boulevard. And the death which had come to it.

"Jesus..."

It was all I could say when the horror came into view. It was not simply 'a lot' of bodies—it was hundreds. Men. Women. Children. Lying in groups along the sidewalk and in the street, a large number congregated around one of the flatbed trucks which was parked near the bank. A pair of bodies were sprawled upon it, a large box open between them.

"Can you get lower?" I asked. "And make another pass?"

"Absolutely," Beekman said.

He turned and set up another run just above the street, hardly a hundred feet above the ground now, less space between our aircraft and the tops of buildings. It was close enough now that, with the binoculars, I could see more clearly what the box had contained.

Pills. Bottles of them, the empty containers strewn about, bright red capsules spilled in several places near bodies. I could also make out the glint of shell casings on the ground, and rifles which had been dropped once their users had succumbed to the now obvious poisoning.

It was a murder suicide. Mostly the latter, with the former reserved for those who had not gone along willingly.

"It's like Jonestown down there," I said, lowering the binoculars, not wanting to see anymore.

Like the cult which had decimated itself by drinking cyanide-laced fruit punch in the jungles of Guyana back in the late 70s. Those people had followed their leader into the abyss. Here, it seemed to me that, without their leader, all the survivors from Yuma saw was an abyss.

"You can schedule with the Council when to come back for Dave's body," I said. "There's no threat left here."

"Right," Beekman said, no joy in his acknowledgment. "Right."

He advanced the throttle and eased the yoke back, gaining altitude and turning us toward home. There would be relief in what we would report, but no joy. Perkins had held his people together too well. In this insane world, they'd accepted his promises, and the premise that they were based upon—that only he could bring them to a better place.

I could only hope that now, somehow, most of those we were leaving behind had found that peace despite their leader's hollow assurances.

Thirty Seven

Johnny Tartek...

It took me a while to understand why Neil would choose the name of a high school football rival of ours to be his last words to me. A somewhat long while. Two weeks and two days, actually.

Then, one evening, while Elaine and I sat with Hope in our living room watching an old kids' movie on the scavenged television hooked to a scavenged DVD player, I remembered. I remembered *The Hit*.

Grace had referenced it obliquely when I mentioned the name, but I hadn't connected that incident to anything meaningful. But meaning there was in it.

'I can take him down...'

That was what Neil had told me, and then told our coach, when Tartek, a lineman of substantial talent and mass, had started to decimate our offensive line. I was at the center position in that game, and Neil was in his usual spot as tight end. He had speed, but he also had guts. Too many, at times.

It was a 'message' play that Coach Macklin allowed. A sweep right behind the line that would put Neil on a collision course with the bull named Tartek. And a collision it was, reminiscent of an eighteen-wheeler t-boning a compact car in an intersection. The bigger player was knocked off course, allowing our running back to slip past for a game-winning touchdown. Neil, though, ricocheted off the impact like a pinball, landing hard on his left side and getting up slowly.

Johnny Tartek...

I understood now what that name was—my friend's final gift to me.

"I have something to do," I said, looking to Elaine.

"Something to do?"

I nodded at her very obvious curiosity, our daughter obliviously fixated on the movie.

"What?" Elaine pressed me.

"Is it all right if I say I'll tell you later?"

It was her turn to nod, a signal of trust that transcended her puzzlement. I stood, planting a kiss on our daughter's head and one on my wife's cheek.

"Don't wait up," I said.

Elaine's curiosity piqued at that, but she didn't press me for any explanation. She let me do what I had to do, and go where I had to go.

* * *

"Excuse me?"

That was Clay Genesee's reaction when I stopped by the hospital and asked to speak to him privately. He'd likely suspected it was some medical issue that I wanted to keep confidential. In a way, it was.

"Grace can't know," I said.

Genesee leaned back against the desk in his small office and crossed his arms over his white coat, considering me with a mix of wonder and disgust.

"Number one, why would I tell her?" he said. "And number two, what purpose would exhuming that man's body serve?"

The marker bearing Neil's name had already been stripped from the spot we'd buried the man we'd believed was him, and had been replaced with one bearing the name of Riley Grimes. But I had to know, and Neil's final words to me had planted the morsel of information that would assuage the doubt he'd noticed in his dying moments.

"In high school Neil took a hard hit in football from a guy named Johnny Tartek," I said. "It actually broke his arm, but he didn't tell anyone but me. He didn't want to miss the next game, which was the last game of the season. The final game of our senior year. Only after that game did he tell his father and go to the doctor. It was a bad fracture, and it was made worse by his stubbornness."

"As I can understand," Genesee said.

"That break would still be obvious," I said. "Wouldn't it? If you took an x-ray or looked beneath the skin?"

Now the man realized fully what I was asking. He was even less enthused than when he was ignorant of my desire.

"There are ethical issues here, Fletch. And legal ones. I'm not saying things like this are never done, but that's in the old world with courts and subpoenas and procedures."

"And we have none of that, Clay. This is me asking you. I have to know for sure."

"You think the imposter might have died out there with you?"

"No," I said, shaking my head. "I don't. But Neil knew enough that there'd always be a part of me that would wonder. Maybe not now, but down the road it might bubble up. That doubt."

"How did he know?"

"Because he knew me better than anyone," I said. "He used his last words to point me toward the answer that would prove it one way or the other."

"Something about this old injury," Clay said.

I nodded. Genesee said nothing, just staring at me for a long moment.

"It's not grave robbing, Clay," I said to break the silence.

"A flip comment isn't going to convince me, Fletch."

"What will?"

He looked off for a moment, seeming to consider not just what I'd asked, but what any action on his part in response to that would say about him. It was a personal struggle the former Naval officer was working through. He'd come from a system of rules and regimentation, but, in the end, he'd chafed at the strictures of that life. Leaving it had, in my opinion, allowed the person who Clay Genesee was meant to be to flourish.

Rules, he'd come to realize, and to accept, weren't made to be broken—they were made by men, all of whom were dead. Those who mattered were not. And I was one of those lucky few.

"Tell me this will put him to rest for you," Genesee said.

I considered that. He wasn't asking me to forget my friend—only to let him exist in memory, not in wonderings.

"It will," I said.

Genesee accepted that with a nod.

"All right," he said. "Let's make this happen."

Thirty Eight

It was just shy of midnight when we reached the top of the coffin scavenged from a funeral parlor up the coast in Coos Bay, both of us having taken turns digging for nearly two hours. I spent five minutes clearing the lid so that the upper half could be lifted open.

I didn't particularly care to see what was inside.

"Climb out, Fletch," Genesee said.

It was his call, and I was happy to oblige. I lifted myself from the rectangular cut we'd made in the earth, most of the coffin's lower half still covered. Bandon's sole doctor climbed down in and motioned for me to pass him a small medical bag he'd brought along. He reached in and retrieved a pair of heavy rubber gloves, slipping into them before straddling the lid and reaching down. A solid tug released the upper half and, by the light of his headlamp and the flashlight I was holding above, he opened the coffin to reveal the decaying face of the man I'd believed was my friend.

I hoped that, after this endeavor, that misplaced belief would still hold true.

Genesee reached into his bag again, one gloved hand coming out wielding a sharp scalpel, its blade gleaming in the artificial light.

"The left radius?" Genesee asked, seeking confirmation of what I'd shared about Neil's injury.

"Left forearm," I answered. "I don't know which bone."

"It'll be the radius," Genesee said as he bent forward and shifted the corpse's left arm to lay upon its abdomen. "I'd bet it won't be the ulna."

I tried not to look, but the face, wasted away to a ghoulish mockery of what had once been human, still bore a resemblance to my friend. What I saw there, lying still in the coffin, could have been him. We were here to prove, for my benefit, that it was not.

"You don't have to watch this, Fletch."

Genesee was suggesting that I turn away as he pulled the sleeve of the suit we'd scrounged, believing we were burying Neil Moore in it. He rotated the loose arm inward, exposing the placement of the bone in question, small pops of old tissue and tendons sounding.

"You do what you've gotta do," I told the doctor.

He did just that, and I watched, the scalpel sawing back and forth through the leathery skin, creating an eight-inch-long incision that Genesee reached his fingers into, spreading the wound open wide. He moved his head back and forth, adjusting the aim of his headlamp into the opening, fingers probing along the bone now exposed within. Within a minute he stopped, easing back to crouch and look up to me.

"There's no break in that bone," Genesee said. "In either bone. I checked both the radius and the ulna. This man never injured his left arm."

I actually let out an audible breath, relief washing over me.

"You're good now?" Genesee asked.

"I'm good now," I confirmed.

There was no more mystery surrounding my friend's death, even if there was plenty that still colored his life. Those wonderings, though, would have to remain just that. No more avenues remained to seek the truths which had gone to the grave with Neil Moore.

All that remained was to bring him home.

Thirty Nine

Two weeks after confirming that the body we'd buried years ago was not that of my friend, I was at the dock ready to step onto the right-side pontoon of Chris Beekman's newly outfitted float plane when a voice stopped me.

Grace's voice.

"Fletch..."

I looked to her, then to Beekman, giving him a signal that I'd be just a minute. He'd been ready to start the Cessna's engine and taxi with me aboard into a position for a water takeoff on the Coquille River. That could wait, though. I would always afford Grace the time when she needed it.

"How are you, Grace?"

"My first day off from the hospital in three weeks," she said. "All the planning to divide supplies and training people for the new settlements. It's been a bit crazy."

In just over a month the first group of settlers would head out to occupy a site twenty-five miles to the south on the coast near Port Orford. Without a full time doctor or nurse on site, volunteers among the seventy slated to move would need to know the basics of suturing wounds and setting broken bones. Much of that had fallen to Grace to administer, and she'd done an amazing job by all accounts.

But that wasn't the only reason she was weary. Old lies had been shattered, and new truths revealed, and amongst that all she'd had to be told that the man she'd married and buried hadn't been dead at all. But now was. On its own that was enough to test any individual. Combined with her self-imposed workload, I truly didn't know how she managed.

"You're going to bring him home," she said, glancing past me to the long basket and straps fixed atop the right pontoon.

The prior week in Beekman's other Cessna a recovery team had been flown in to retrieve Dave Arndt's body. He was buried in the town cemetery the following day with nearly the entire population in attendance. It was now my friend's turn to be returned to where those who cared for him could be near.

"It should only take five or six hours," I told her. "We'll be back before dark."

She nodded and said nothing for a moment, the silence seeming prelude to something. As it turned out, it was.

"I want to come with you," Grace said. "I talked it over with Clay and he encouraged me to do it."

It was her right, I believed, to accompany us to retrieve the remains of her former husband. But that didn't mean it was a good idea. Inside the aircraft was a body bag and shovels. Exhuming a body, I'd learned, was not for the faint of heart. And when that body was a loved one, I knew it was going to be difficult for me. I didn't know if Grace could handle it.

"And trying to talk me out of it won't work," she said, her prescience cutting off any attempt to dissuade her. "I understand the realities of what has to be done to get him into that basket."

"You're sure about this, Grace?"

"I owe this to him, Fletch. And to myself."

* * *

An hour later, after an uneventful takeoff from the smooth waters of the Coquille River, we descended toward Medicine Lake.

"It's beautiful here," Grace said through the headset.

She sat behind Beekman on the left side of the aircraft. I looked back to her from the front passenger seat and saw her gaze fixed on the landscape below. Much of it was grey, but in the midst of that was the bolt of blue water. To the north the ancient volcanic terrain was hued with blacks and reds.

"From up here it's just so…"

"Peaceful," I said.

She looked to me and smiled.

* * *

Beekman put us down with hardly a splash and taxied toward a sandy beach at the east end of the lake. He cut the engine and coasted until the front of the pontoons bottomed out on the silty bottom of the shallows. I climbed out first and helped Grace, a short hop putting us both on dry land without getting wet. Beekman passed the shovels and body bag over, then joined us on shore, anchoring the aircraft to a solid stump thirty feet from the lake's edge.

"It's up about a quarter mile above the north side of the lake," I told Grace and Beekman.

"Fletch, can I just see the spot before…"

She didn't need to specify the remainder of her request. Soon we would, in essence, be defiling the grave where the man she'd loved had been buried after falling in battle. Where he'd fallen after ending Perkins' miserable life so that I could return to my wife, and to my child.

"If you could just show me where it is," Grace requested.

"Of course," I said, looking to Beekman.

"I'll just hang back until you're ready," he said, offering a quiet smile to Grace.

"Thank you," she said.

I stepped away from the shore and reached my hand back toward her.

"Come on," I said.

She put her hand in mine and I led her into the grey woods.

* * *

It took twenty minutes to navigate the meandering path through the old pine forest, half of which had fallen, leaving rotting logs to climb over or duck under.

"It's so quiet here," Grace said as I helped her through a tangle of twisted limbs. "A different quiet than other places we've been."

She and Neil had traveled with Krista across the country when it reeked of death soon after the blight. I understood what she meant about there being something to differentiate this peacefulness from that absence of noise.

"It is," I said.

We reached the spot where Neil Moore had been buried, the sun high in the bright blue sky. Grace approached the makeshift marker I'd made. She crouched and let her fingers trace along the rough carving of letters and numbers that signified the thinnest tale of the man. Name and the dates of when he came into this world, and when he left it.

"It's probably terrible to say, but I'm glad you were with him, Fletch."

"It's not terrible," I said. "And I am glad I was there."

She stood straight again and looked out from the spot where her former husband lay beneath a few feet of earth. There was no cool green grass here to sooth the spot of its inherent sorrow. No bright flowers or scent of blooms. No chirping birds to distract. Someday there might be, but my friend would not be here for those changes which the slowly healing earth would eventually allow.

On that fact, I was about to be proven wrong.

"Look at the world in the lake," Grace said. "It all looks better in reflection."

I had to admit, she was right. The glassy water hued the barren landscape with a pleasing blue aura, colors from the sky drizzled in to paint the scene as only an artist could on canvas. Here, though, it was real, and it was mesmerizing.

Grace turned away from the view and looked to me, smiling lightly.

"I want to leave him here," she said.

I didn't counter her statement, though I did take a single step toward her.

"Grace, are you sure?"

She nodded, a surety about her. A contentment.

"If I can make that decision, then I say yes," she said, looking back toward the grave and the shimmering lake beyond. "He deserves to be at peace in a peaceful place. I don't know that there is any place that could match this."

I took in the same sight that she was, and I could not argue her point. Nor would I. I agreed with her, though it took this visit to my friend's grave to even consider that this was the place where he should rest for all eternity.

"I think this is right," I said. "We can bring the stone marker when it's finished and have it placed."

She nodded, still smiling, though now a skim of tears began to glisten in her eyes. I eased her into a side hug and held her close, her head tipping against my shoulder as we looked together at the spot my friend and her love would remain forever.

Forty

We flew back to Bandon and landed on the babbling Coquille River before taxiing to the dock past boats moored in the harbor. Elaine, Schiavo, and Martin were waiting for us.

Something was wrong.

"A welcome party," I commented as I stepped onto the pontoon and helped Grace from the plane.

"We need to talk," Martin said.

It was curious that he was the one to speak, I thought. Not Elaine, the civilian leader of Bandon, nor Schiavo, the former military leader who now served as advisor on those matters to the Town Council. Martin was as much an outsider as I was, though we were both pulled into the necessities of serving the town frequently.

"Is everything all right?" Grace asked.

Beekman slipped past her and tied the plane off to the dock. He noticed the reception committee's silence when the question was posed to them. Grace, though, wisely knew not to press the issue, and leaned down to give Elaine a quick hug before excusing herself.

"Clay and the kids will want to hear what we decided," she said, then flashed me a smile tinged with a hint of concern and walked past those who'd met us and disappeared past the end of the dock.

"What did you decide?" Schiavo asked.

"He's staying there," I told her. "Now what's going on?"

"Our car's in the lot," Martin said. "We'll talk on the way."

He didn't want to say any more. None of them did. I suspected it was because we were not entirely alone. Chris Beekman didn't take any offense at the obvious withholding of information and went about removing the empty stretcher basket from the pontoon.

"Chris, thanks," I said.

He gave me a thumbs up and continued with his work. I slung my M4 and pushed Elaine's chair out to the lot. I stowed her chair in the trunk and climbed into the back seat next to her, Schiavo at the wheel next to her husband.

"Okay, what's going on?" I asked.

The retired Army colonel started the car and steered us out of the lot, letting the town's former leader share what had happened. What was still happening. I listened but said little, wanting to see for myself what he had described. Needing to see it with my own eyes so that I might not think this was just some bad dream that had folded itself into a nightmare.

* * *

Jackson Petrie was the one who had found it. He'd called Martin right away out of habit, and the news was passed to those who needed to know, just the four of us so far.

"Anyone else come by?" Martin asked as we approached Jackson.

The drive to the farm fields just east of town a few hundred yards south of the Coquille River had taken less than ten minutes. But in that time it seemed that something else had transpired. I could sense that clearly in Jackson's almost grim demeanor.

"Scott Barnes called," the man reported. "He's seeing it, too."

Elaine looked up to Martin.

"Scott's fields are two miles southeast," she said.

Martin nodded.

"Let's show Fletch," he said.

I pushed Elaine along a gravel path cut through the grow beds and past a stretch of greenhouses, following Jackson, Martin and Schiavo just behind. The man leading us was one of those who ran the town's various farming properties, Scott Barnes and Leticia Lopez the others. Aside from that which the town's residents grew in their own gardens, these massive fields where plants immune to the blight were cultivated and harvested were essential to Bandon's long-term survival. Combined with the seed germination lab in town, an uninterrupted supply of food could be assured.

Until now.

"Over here," Jackson said, pointing off toward a section of corn nearly chest high.

The gravel path did not lead toward the planted rows whose silky ears were more than a month away from harvesting.

"I'll wait here with Jackson," Elaine said. "I've seen enough already."

I could have maneuvered her chair across the uneven dirt, as she could have herself, but I was the one who'd been brought here to see what they already had. Already knowing what that appeared to be from the description they'd shared on the drive over, I wasn't eager to have their fears confirmed by my own eyes.

"I'll wait with Elaine," Jackson said, looking to the three of us. "You go."

* * *

Martin took the lead and guided me and Schiavo between the rows of corn, penetrating more than halfway into the field. The day was creeping toward its end, sun just over my left shoulder and the afternoon breeze kicking up, tossing the gangly corn leaves about.

"It's about fifty feet from the north end of this row," Martin said.

"What does Scott Barnes have growing over at his fields?" Schiavo asked.

"A mix of greens," I said. "Lettuce, cabbage. Potatoes, too, I think."

"Potatoes for sure," Martin confirmed.

We continued on, deeper into the dense acreage which had been reclaimed from the blighted fields. The information Neil and Elaine and I had brought back from our mission to Cheyenne had allowed all this to happen. A solitary academic working in an underground lab had discovered the cure for the agricultural bioweapon that had ravaged the once green earth. His work, which he hadn't lived to see bear both literal and metaphoric fruit, was on display here for all to see.

But there was something more to see. Something new. And unwelcome.

"It's right—"

Martin was pointing just ahead toward the row of corn plants hemming us in on the right. But he stopped, speaking and walking, as something caught his eye. His hand came down and he looked back to me and Schiavo.

"It was further up three hours ago," he said.

I stepped past him, brushing against the stalks and flapping leaves. A few steps brought me to what had stopped Martin in his tracks, and what had brought me here as the day wound down.

Spots.

They were grey and bore no distinct shape, some circular while others stretched out like ashen, dusty veins upon the surface of the plants. A gust of wind raised a puff of nearly colorless grit from where the blemishes had appeared on this plant, and on others.

Stretching from this southern end of the spreading infection, I could see dozens of the once bountiful plants beginning to wilt before my eyes. Stalks which should be strong and straight were leaning into the narrow space between the rows, making contact with nearby plants.

"It's spreading," Martin said. "Fast."

He was talking about something I'd witnessed before, looking out from my refuge across the valley to the lush slopes of mountains to the east. In the course of hours I'd watched the vibrant mountainsides turn from the loveliest of colors to a sickly grey pallor.

The same pallor I was seeing now.

"The blight's back," Schiavo said.

I reached out and felt the infected plant nearest me. It bent easily in my grip, whatever had afflicted it in the previous hours already ravaging its internal structure.

"We have to isolate these fields," she said. "Burn them if necessary."

I snapped the top of the corn stalk off in my hand, letting it crumble into brittle bits and fall to the fouled earth below as I looked to Schiavo and shook my head.

"It won't matter," I said. "It's too late."

"He's not wrong," Martin said, directing his wife's attention to the parallel rows near the blighted stalks.

"Dear God," Schiavo said quietly as she saw what he had.

The blight had already spread to those rows, the first bits of the hellish grey infection spotting stalk and leaf and silk. This corn crop was lost.

As was much more.

* * *

We left the corn field and returned to where Elaine and Jackson waited. Only my wife remained there, one of the refurbished cell phones that used the town's self-engineered network in hand.

"Where did Jackson go?"

"Letty called," she said.

Letty was Leticia Lopez, another farm manager. Her fields were mostly dedicated to beans and wheat and smaller vegetables like tomatoes and onions. What she had called about I didn't expect to be surprised by.

"It's there, too," Elaine told us.

No one said anything for a moment, this new and old impediment to our survival leaving little that could be offered, other than more dreadful truths.

"By morning it will be in every backyard garden in town," I said. "The seedlings that were planted are probably already showing signs."

"Has anyone checked the orchards?" Elaine asked.

"It's not necessary," I told her. "It's there. It's everywhere."

Everywhere except...

I grabbed the phone from my wife and dialed from memory, a three-digit extension all that was needed to ring any of the two hundred handsets in use. It rang in my ear, once, then twice.

"Who are you calling?" Schiavo asked.

"Seed processing," Krista answered.

The young girl, fourteen now, had taken a job as clerk at the germination lab where plants were cultivated and seeds were harvested from the immune stock. It was only three days a week, time spent mostly handing out packets of seeds to farmers and home gardeners who'd placed orders, either in person or over the phone.

"Krista, let me talk to Willy," I said.

Willy Kellridge ran the germination lab and had, almost singlehandedly, sped up the processing of seeds from young plants, a necessity to sustain and expand the town's farming operations. His background in chemistry didn't perfectly suit the forty-year-old for the position, but his quick intellect did, allowing him to create entirely new botanical processes from scratch.

"He's not here," Krista answered. "He was taking today off to look for rocks and shells down at the beach. I think he wants to grind the shells up for fertilizer, or something."

What she'd just shared wasn't what I'd wanted to hear. Until it was.

"Have you been there alone all day, Krista?"

"Yep. I even opened up. Willy gave me the keys and—"

"Lock the door," I told her. "Lock it and don't open it until I tell you, understand?"

I could hear a soft, frightened gasp at the other end.

"Fletch, what's wrong?"

"Has anyone been in today?" I asked the teen girl.

"Ju-just one person this morning to drop off an order," Krista reported. "Fletch, please, what's—"

"Krista, you have to trust me," I said. "It will be all right. Now, have you left the building today?"

"No," she said. "I brought my lunch and I...I just stayed in and did paperwork for Willy."

"You didn't take a step outside? Not for anything?"

"No," she said. "Not a step."

"Okay," I said, easing myself toward a place of calm for her sake. "I'll be there in a few minutes. Lock the door. I'll call your mom and let her know what's going on."

"Okay," Krista said, steeling herself as much as any fourteen-year-old could.

"Be right there."

I ended the call and handed the phone back to Elaine just as Jackson came jogging up.

"It's in town," he said, breathing hard. "Rob Oldham is over at the tractor shed saying his raspberry bushes are covered in grey ash."

Schiavo looked to me, then to Elaine.

"That's north, east, and south," the military advisor said, providing information to the town's leader as well as simply speaking to a friend. "It's coming from all sides."

Elaine nodded and thought for a moment.

"Eric, I know you said it doesn't matter, but we need to know how far it's pushed into the plantings we've done in the woods," Elaine said.

"If it's here, it's going to blow right through there," I said.

"I still want to know," she countered.

It was her call to make. I could see the logic in the desire and the decision, but in a normal situation. This was not that. We'd all experienced this scenario before as the blight swept over the entire planet. If it was back, it wasn't likely that it was any less potent than its first appearance.

In all likelihood, it would be more.

"Where did it come from?" Elaine asked, frustrated.

"Here," Jackson told her. "It never left. It's been in the soil, the trees."

"Why now?" Elaine pressed. "We've had almost perfect crops for years."

"We can figure that out later," I interjected. "The only thing that matters right now is securing the seeds that haven't been exposed to any of this."

"That's why you wanted Krista to lock the germination lab down," Schiavo said.

I nodded. It was a gut reaction, one that would have come to others eventually, but it had bubbled up in my thoughts first.

"She's got to be scared after that call," Martin said.

"I'll call Grace for you, Fletch," Schiavo said, taking her own cell from her pocket and dialing as she started back toward the car.

"Jackson, we've got to go," Elaine said. "I'll keep you updated."

The farmer nodded, but it seemed more an acceptance of some awful fate than simple acknowledgment. There was fear in his eyes. The kind of fear I'd seen in people who were facing a terrible unknown.

The truth was, it wasn't an unknown. And we were all facing it. Again.

Forty One

We locked down the germination lab and posted guards to secure it after bringing Krista out. Willy was snatched from his foray to the beaches south of town and brought to the site just after dark, confirming what we wanted to hear— that the vault holding the immune seed stock hadn't been opened in weeks. His efforts had been focused on using naturally produced seeds and seedlings in that time, effectively isolating the supply from any mutated contamination which might be causing the resurgence of the blight.

He wasn't certain, though, that we were facing the same kind of threat.

"It could be generational," he told the Town Council, which had been gathered for an emergency meeting that both Martin and I were asked to sit in on. "Just like the initial discovery that ultraviolet-b radiation in sunlight was the catalyst which supercharged the rapid spread of the blight, the immunity could be something that is deprecated after a certain number of generations."

"Is that available in English?" Stu Parker asked.

"The immunity gets less and less after each plant produces seeds," I said, annoyed. "Momma plant produces seeds with less resistance to the blight than it. Baby plant produces seeds with even less resistance. And so on. Is that clear enough for you, Stu?"

Elaine fixed an annoyed gaze of her own on me and I settled back into the chair I'd taken next to Schiavo. I wasn't sure if it was Stu's grating nature at the moment, or the mere fact that it was sinking in what we were facing. In a way it was the worst possible thing to deal with as a community. Volcanic eruptions and malevolent military forces we'd overcome. This, though, was a repeat of the very thing which had nearly wiped the planet clean of all life.

This second go round might finish the job.

"So the seeds in the vault won't matter?" Hannah asked the man charged with protecting them.

"No, they very well could be the key to getting past this," Willy said. "Fletch was right to lock them down."

"Could," Elaine said, parroting the man's qualifier.

Willy nodded and shrugged.

"We're in uncharted territory here," the man told the Council.

Elaine looked around the room and rolled her chair back from the table, turning so that she could reach a map which was prominent on the wall. On it was Bandon and the surrounding area stretching almost to the settlement at Remote. She pointed at that spot where more than a hundred people now resided.

"Remote isn't reporting any signs of blight yet," she said. "Camas Valley, either. That's from communications twenty minutes ago. But I'm guessing from what we've heard and seen that that's going to change."

"If failure is built into the seeds we've produced, then it will affect them," Willy confirmed.

Something, though, struck me right then. More curiosity than question, at first. Within a few seconds, though, as the wondering churned fast in my thoughts, it became a full on imperative to understand.

"Why?"

Those gathered for the meeting looked to me.

"Why aren't they reporting anything?" I asked. "They have seeds planted from the same stock that we do, at the same time."

"Remote planted even earlier," Martin said, catching on to what I was getting at. "They wanted to get a jump on the growing season."

Attention shifted from me and Martin to Willy, who seemed to be intensely pondering the inconsistency I'd just pointed out.

"Willy?" Elaine prodded the man.

"I don't know," he said. "We're only a few hours into this. I'd need to check the fields at Remote and Camas Valley and verify what they're seeing."

Before any agreement could be offered to that suggestion, Schiavo spoke up.

"That may not be a good idea," she said.

"Why?" Joel Matthews asked her.

She stood and moved to the same map that Elaine sat near in her wheelchair, pointing to several points.

"The three farming operations are hit," Schiavo said. "Gardens here, and here, and here, and, well, basically everywhere."

In the hours after the resurgence of the blight had taken everyone by surprise, dozens of home gardens had been reported as affected. It was accepted that, by morning, a survey would show that the impending damage would be one-hundred percent.

"We know that," Elaine said. "Why shouldn't Willy confirm what's going on inland?"

Schiavo took a moment and looked to each of those around the table. For some reason, when she'd finished, her gaze settled on me.

"Because what if the problem is us," she said.

She still looked at me, the woman, the leader, who'd faced all that there was to be faced in battle, and more. I'd been witness to those acts, by her side during some of the most intense moments either of us had faced. And I'd watched her change, from a junior Army officer thrust into chaos to a full Colonel being handed the ultimate destructive power by the President of the United States. We understood each other. That was why she had fixed on me, I believed, because what she was suggesting was painful to even consider. In war, in a fight for one's life, though, hard truths had to be faced before they could be overcome.

"You mean something here," Elaine said, and Schiavo nodded.

"We have to consider that," I said.

Elaine thought for a moment, then rolled herself back to the table. Schiavo sat again next to her.

"Do we have any people out in the field?" Elaine asked. "Any scouting or scavenging missions?"

"None at the moment," Hannah Morse answered.

"Marv and Ginny Ballis are at the cottage down the coast," Stu shared. "They're due back tomorrow. I mean today."

It was past midnight. A new day had effectively begun. In the dark, in homes across Bandon, worry had risen from a place it had been buried for a while now. Worry and outright fear. Only the youngest of residents, from newborns to children who were toddlers at the time the town was a beacon known as Eagle One, had no memory of the blight and its ravages. Those of us who did were feeling a sickening sense of déjà vu, one that we'd not expected to ever experience again.

But we were.

"Close the roads," Elaine said.

"Wait," Stu said. "This is a Council decision. We have to agree on any—"

"Not under the emergency powers section of the charter," Elaine reminded him.

The documents which formalized Bandon's government after Martin had stepped away from his de facto leadership of the town several years ago included the provision Elaine was invoking, one that could only be overturned should the remaining elected Council members vote unanimously to do so.

That wasn't going to happen.

"Elaine is right," Joel said. "This situation requires action."

Stu shook his head and settled back into his seat.

"I'm not disagreeing with it, I just think if—"

"We don't have time to think and debate," Elaine interrupted him, turning to Schiavo next. "Will you have the garrison set up the required roadblocks and initiate patrols?"

"Lt. Lorenzen will take care of it," she said.

Her former second-in-command, who now led the garrison, would take on the task with his usual measured tenacity. Now, though, he had more teeth to put into any bite that needed to be taken out of the mission.

"I'll have him integrate the Marines into the assignment," Schiavo added.

Though Lorenzen shared his rank with Lt. Mason, an understanding had been reached in just the last twelve hours that command decisions would rest with the Army lieutenant leading the garrison. There was no animosity between the cordially rival service members, only good-natured joking concerning how many of the competing service members it would take to screw in a light bulb, though much cruder versions of the ribbing had clearly been shared. But in this instance, I had no doubt, nor did Schiavo, I was certain, that both units would coalesce around what needed to be done.

"All right," Elaine said.

She gave each person in attendance a final look, gauging reactions to the decisions she'd made. There was no open resistance, not even from Stu Parker. We'd faced crises before, but nothing like this. The first scourge of the blight had wiped out nearly the whole of humanity. Now it was back, and it had taken direct aim at those of us who'd adapted and overcome. And if we couldn't find a way to beat it back once again, we'd soon join our brethren who'd already left this world.

"God help us," Elaine said, ending the meeting with that hope which, in itself, signaled the grim reality we faced.

Forty Two

By noon the next day Bandon was sealed off. Roadblocks had been placed at the north, south, and east entrances to town. The survey of the saplings and orchards planted on the outskirts of town had been completed, confirming that the blight was, in a terrible repeat performance, on its way to wiping out all that we'd struggled to recreate since returning from Cheyenne with the cure.

The cure that was not that at all, it now appeared.

The in-town survey of all things that had been planted was also near completion. Everything from flower beds in the park to vegetable gardens in the backyards of so many homes was being inspected, the degree of damage to each noted for a report to the Town Council.

One report, though, became more urgent than others. Martin's call to me as I stole a few minutes with my daughter at home made that clear.

"Can you meet me at Mrs. DaSilva's house?" he asked me over the phone.

"I have Hope right now," I told him. "I'll need to get—"

"Bring her, Fletch. This can't wait."

I didn't know what had him so worked up, though it could have been any number of things. Panic hadn't set in among Bandon's residents—not fully. But already there was clear worry, and complaints against the town's leaders for letting this happen. That was fear speaking, I knew. Normally rational people lashing out because, deep within, they knew that those who could be blamed were long dead.

It was more venting than complaining, when one looked at the overall situation.

That, though, didn't ease the building tension by any appreciable amount. And there was no telling what tomorrow would bring. Or the next day.

"On my way," I told Martin.

I needed no more explanation from the man, his judgement that my presence was somehow necessary more than enough reason to make that happen. I gathered my daughter up and loaded her in the child seat next to me in the pickup. In just over five minutes I pulled up in front of Noreen DaSilva's house. She was sixty and a blight widow, her husband dying during their journey west from their home in Missouri. Like others, they had followed the beacon to Eagle One, but only she had made it, arriving just before Neil and I had with Grace and Krista. In the years since then her home had been on the south side of town, with woods just a stone's throw from her back porch. As were the greying saplings which, just a day ago, had brimmed with vibrant green needles on strong limbs.

When I pulled up to the curb in front of the woman's house, Martin was waiting at the bottom of the front steps. I wouldn't describe his expression as grim as much as uncertain. That would not have surprised me regarding anyone else, but it did with him. Martin Jay had always been decisive. An action taker. His adeptness at sizing up situations and reacting quickly and appropriately had, in essence, kept Bandon and its residents alive through the worst of the blight. That I now saw in him something unlike that surety was unsettling.

"Come on, sweetie," I said, lifting Hope from her car seat and setting her down on the browning parkway grass next to the sidewalk.

"Uncle Martin!"

She ran toward him, his expression shifting immediately to joyful. The smile was muted, though, and as he picked her up and wrapped her in a hug he looked to me, something more showing through his gaze now—confusion.

"Oh, you brought my favorite little helper!" Noreen DaSilva said, beaming brightly as she came out of her house and scooped Hope from Martin's arms, my daughter wrapping hers around the genial woman's neck. "I have got some cookies just out of the oven that need tasting."

Noreen looked to me, as did my daughter, and I gave a quick nod. The grandmotherly woman lowered Hope to the walkway and took her tiny hand, leading her into the house.

"What is it, Martin?" I asked once we were alone.

He gestured toward the side of the house and led me that way, down the path to the back yard, where Mrs. DaSilva's beloved greenhouse sat behind her residence and the detached garage. Martin went to the opaque structure, layers of plastic covering its metal skin, trapping heat and moisture within to foster plant growth. The woman had bred a dozen varieties of tomatoes from seed, sharing nearly all with neighbors and friends. Her green thumb was well known, but even it could not stop the scourge which had come again to our world. As Martin opened the flimsy door I could see rows of drooping grey stalks even before entering, the blight infecting this collection of greenery as it had all others.

"It's like the rest, Martin," I said. "Why show me this?"

He shook his head and closed the greenhouse door behind us.

"Noreen called me a while ago," he said. "She wanted me to see something before the survey team got to her house."

"See what?" I asked.

He stepped toward the rear of the greenhouse and stopped at the end of one long planting table, its bed three feet off the ground. Plants that were vibrant just the day before were lying limp and ashen upon the soil beds.

"She was afraid there might be some reaction," Martin said. "Against her."

"Why?"

"People get strange ideas when under stress," he said. "Mob mentality can set in when something that should be one way isn't. They can easily blame a person for difficulties they're facing."

"Martin, what are you talking about?" I pressed him.

He looked to his left and reached down behind the planting table, gripping something with one hand before lifting it into view and placing it on a patch of bare soil. It was a pot, one like many others scattered about the greenhouse, a plant in it also like the others.

Except this plant was green and straight, standing tall, very unlike every other bit of flora that surrounded it. That surrounded us.

"One plant in the entire town that's unaffected," Martin said. "A tomato plant. And I'm willing to say I'm feeling a bit of déjà vu right now."

I understood what he meant, even if I could not comprehend the circumstances at the moment. The image of a living, thriving tomato plant broadcast over an amateur television signal had drawn us to Cheyenne in search of a cure for the blight. We'd crossed the wastelands to find that very thing and had returned with it. All because of a green plant not unlike what Martin had summoned me to see.

"There are no spots on it," he said. "It's been right next to everything else in here and it's still green."

I approached the plant and felt its leaves. They were soft and sturdy, unlike the withered examples next to it. It was alive. As alive as it was twenty-four hours ago. But would it still be once twenty-four more had passed?

"I know what you're thinking, Fletch—maybe it's just a delayed reaction. Tomorrow it will be like every other plant in and around Bandon. But that makes as much sense as its current condition. It shouldn't be like this. It's no different than these other plants."

"Except it is," I said.

"Except it is," Martin agreed. "And my money would be on it being green and strong tomorrow."

I stepped back and surveyed the carnage in the greenhouse, then looked to Bandon's former leader and, in many ways, its savior.

"Noreen thinks people will yell 'witch' when they find out?"

"It's happened before," Martin reminded me.

"It's not going to stay quiet," I told him.

"I know," he said. "But the information has to be shared *by* the town."

"The Council, you mean," I prompted him.

He nodded.

"And just what do you think they can say that won't just freak people out more than they already are?" I asked.

Before he even spoke, the obvious answer to my own question bubbled to the surface in my thoughts. The guiding principal of almost everything I'd done since leaving Montana.

"They can say that this shows there is hope," Martin said, pointing to the surviving tomato plant.

Some would accept that. Would believe it. Most, maybe. But for the first time in a very long time, I wasn't convinced that a belief that all would turn out well would be enough. In my own heart, I had to admit, I was having doubts.

I was truly fearful that we didn't have much time left.

Thank You

I hope you enjoyed *Destroyer*. Please look for other books in *The Bugging Out Series*.

About The Author

Noah Mann lives in the West and has been involved in personal survival and disaster preparedness for more than two decades. He has extensive training in firearms, as well as urban and wilderness Search & Rescue operations, including tracking and the application of technology in victim searches.

97568964R00150

Made in the USA
Lexington, KY
30 August 2018